MRS. PARGETER'S POUND OF FLESH

Also by Simon Brett
in Thorndike Large Print ®

Mrs., Presumed Dead

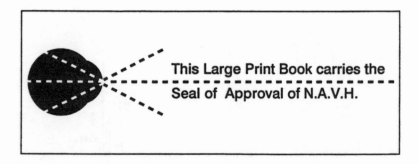

This Large Print Book carries the
Seal of Approval of N.A.V.H.

MRS. PARGETER'S POUND OF FLESH

A MRS. PARGETER MYSTERY

SIMON BRETT

Thorndike Press • Thorndike, Maine

Thorndike Large Print ® Cloak & Dagger Series edition published in 1993 by arrangement with Charles Scribner's Sons.

The tree indicium is a trademark of Thorndike Press.

Set in 16 pt. News Plantin by Juanita Macdonald.

This book is printed on acid-free, high opacity paper. ∞

Library of Congress Cataloging in Publication Data

Brett, Simon.
   Mrs. Pargeter's pound of flesh : a Mrs. Pargeter mystery / Simon Brett.
      p.   cm.
   ISBN 1-56054-771-5 (alk. paper : lg. print)
   1. Pargeter, Mrs. (Fictitious character)—Fiction. 2. Women detectives—England—Fiction. 3. Large type books. I. Title.
   PR6052.R4296M38   1993b
   823'.914—dc20   93-17745
                                                            CIP

TO PENNY AND ANTHONY

Chapter One

'Eleven stone three pounds.' There was only a hint of intonation in the girl's voice as the digital display of the weighing machine settled. It was an intonation that could have inspired guilt and the resolve to slim in a susceptible person.

Mrs Pargeter was not such a person. 'Yes, that's about right,' she said comfortably in her cockney-tinged accent as she stepped off the platform.

'There are a few other measurements we take for all new arrivals at Brotherton Hall,' the white-uniformed girl, whose plastic name-badge identified her as 'Lindy Galton', recited from a much-repeated script. 'Bust, waist, hips, obviously, and height . . .'

'Why, you haven't got any treatment that can change people's height, have you?' asked Mrs Pargeter curiously.

The girl coloured. 'Well, no . . .'

'Good. Because the only ones I've heard of to do that are decapitation and the rack, and I don't think either is a recommended health spa practice, is it?'

Lindy Galton looked at the older woman uncertainly. She wasn't used to such behaviour from new arrivals. Plenty of them made nervous jokes about their outlines or proportions as they mounted the scales, but few demonstrated this kind of comfortable good humour. And few, come to that, accepted with such equanimity the confirmation that they were overweight. By definition, most arrivals at a health spa are dissatisfied with their bodies; yet this new woman, this plump and white-haired Mrs Pargeter, seemed to inhabit hers with tranquillity and even delight.

The friend, though, a frizzy natural blonde in her late forties, who was even now stripping off her Brotherton Hall towelling gown to step on to the scales, reacted in a much more traditional way. 'I'm afraid there's rather a lot of me,' she giggled as she shook off her flip-flops. 'Mrs Cellulite, my oldest daughter calls me.'

This woman, 'Kim Thurrock' according to the details on Lindy Galton's clipboard, had a much less serious weight problem than her friend, but it worried her a lot more. Abstractedly, Lindy noted a roll of fat above the knicker line, some flabbiness in the thighs and upper arms, but no worse than on the average female body that has survived forty-eight years and borne three children. Lindy spent her working life looking at such bodies and had never been judgemental about them, even though few compared to her own finely tuned and finely toned instrument.

The health spa — latest incarnation of many for the splendid eighteenth-century Brotherton Hall — only accepted female 'guests'. And the owner of Brotherton Hall, Mr Arkwright, insisted that all his female staff had perfect bodies. This was not for his own benefit — Mr Arkwright was punctiliously correct in such matters, never guilty of the mildest verbal sexism or ambiguous pat on a passing buttock — it was simply a marketing ploy.

Mr Arkwright knew he ran a business founded on guilt and envy; and he knew that the perfect physical condition of his female staff was bound to stimulate both in his customers, leading them to spend more time and money in pursuit of comparable excellence. Mr Arkwright had been called many things in his varied career, but never a fool.

Mrs Pargeter looked at her friend, giggling self-consciously on the platform. Even though nearly twenty years her senior, Mrs Pargeter had always felt a great affinity to Kim. The younger woman's husband, known universally as 'Thicko' Thurrock, had been an associate of the late Mr Pargeter, and the two women had met frequently at functions connected with the business.

Mrs Pargeter spent a lot of time at the Thurrocks' tiny house in Catford. Contentedly childless herself, she had taken great interest in the arrival and development of the Thurrocks' three daughters, and was always enthusiastically welcomed at the house by the family's poodles. She had found Kim's company and sympathy invaluable when Mr Pargeter died.

There had always been a bond of willing obligation between the two women, and so when Kim Thurrock let slip the fact that she was worried about her weight, Mrs Pargeter had been only too happy to fix up the three days at Brotherton Hall.

She had also been fully prepared to fund the visit. The late Mr Pargeter had left his widow lavishly provided for, and she was always happy to help out a friend in less comfortable circumstances.

As it transpired, however, payment at Brotherton Hall was not required. Mr Arkwright (known at earlier stages of his career as 'Ankle-Deep' Arkwright from the habit of dipping his toe into a great variety of endeavours) was another associate of the late Mr Pargeter and, once he had recovered from his delight at hearing from his former boss's widow and understood her request, would not hear of — indeed, was deeply offended by the suggestion of — any money changing hands.

'After all your husband done for me, Mrs P,' (in moments of emotion the manicured syntax with which he greeted visitors to Brotherton Hall might occasionally lapse), 'it's the very least I could do for you. Stay a week, stay a fortnight, stay a month, bring all the friends you've got! Be my pleasure to look after you.'

So once again Mrs Pargeter had had reason to be grateful for the late Mr Pargeter's most precious legacy — his address-book, a compendium of contacts which could procure a surprising range of unconventional services.

She was particularly glad to be able to help Kim, because of the younger woman's unfortunate circumstances. These were only in part financial. Her husband, Thicko Thurrock, was a man of great warmth and gentleness, but it was not for nothing that he had earned his nickname. While benefiting from the wise tutelage of the late Mr Pargeter he had been well protected, but, with the death of his mentor, soon found himself mixing in less savoury areas of business and with less savoury associates.

It was from then only a matter of time before something went wrong. Something did, outside a branch of the Halifax Building Society in Clerkenwell, and Thicko Thurrock was invited to spend seven years as a guest of Her Majesty Queen Elizabeth the Second (though not at Buckingham Palace — and the invitation's RSVP had not offered the option of refusal).

Mrs Pargeter had watched with increasing admiration the effort Kim Thurrock put into keeping the family together during her husband's unavoidable absence; but it was clear as the end of the seven years drew near that Kim was increasingly uneasy at the prospect of Thicko's return.

The minimum of probing had identified the problem. There was nothing basically wrong with the relationship — the couple still adored each other — but Kim Thurrock had totally lost confidence in her continuing sexual attractiveness. No amount of reassurance could persuade her away from the conviction that seven years had changed her into 'an old boot' and that her husband, on his return to the marital nest, would take one careful look at what was on offer there before immediately walking out to shack up with a twenty-year-old.

Mrs Pargeter had tried every argument she knew, the main one being that Thicko wasn't that kind of man, but to no avail. Kim's self-esteem had sunk too low to be resuscitated by logic. More extreme measures would be needed.

It was at this point that Mrs Pargeter had thought of Ankle-Deep Arkwright and Brotherton Hall; and, from the moment she mentioned the idea, she knew she had found the right solution. Kim positively sparkled at the prospect, perhaps not only of losing weight but also of having a break from pampering three small girls, and even of being a little pampered herself.

As Mrs Pargeter looked at her friend giggling girlishly on the weighing machine that Sunday evening, she felt the warm glow of having done the right thing.

Chapter Two

Weekdays or weekends, the evening meal at Brotherton Hall was taken early — at half-past six, which to Mrs Pargeter's mind was no time to be eating an evening meal. Nor did what was put in front of her conform with her definition of what an evening meal should be.

At the centre of a large plate some leaves of lettuce and other subservient greenery abased themselves before a little mound of cottage cheese. Now Mrs Pargeter was a broadminded woman of generous spirit. There were few things in the world that riled her enough to make a fuss; but one of that tiny minority was cottage cheese.

She didn't know whether it was the appearance that offended her most, its close resemblance to what can be seen at the bottom of a just-stirred pot of Non-Drip Brilliant White Vinyl Matt Emulsion; or the slippery nothingness of its touch against her tongue; or the taste, that failed aspiration to piquancy and resulting compromise of slight unpleasantness. Probably more than any of these what put Mrs Pargeter off cottage cheese was the expression of sanctimonious righteousness worn by its habitual eaters.

'I'm sorry,' she said. 'I don't think this is right.'

There was nothing peremptory in her tone, just a gentle pointing-out of an error in the menu distribution. The waitress consulted a list. 'You're Mrs Pargeter, aren't you?' And, on receipt of confirmation, 'No, that *is* right. You're on the same diet as Mrs Thurrock.'

'But.' Mrs Pargeter pointed to her plate, confident of the monosyllable's eloquence.

Kim jollied her along. 'Come on, Melita. No slacking. We're in this together. *Il faut souffrir pour être belle.*' (She had taken advantage of the last seven years' enforced solitude to improve her education at evening classes.)

Mrs Pargeter realized she was in a cleft stick (a particularly uncomfortable metaphor for a woman of her ample proportions). Kim had been reluctant to accept charity, and had only agreed to the Brotherton Hall visit when her friend had invented a pretext of needing support in her own battle against excess poundage. Mrs Pargeter was obliged therefore to make at least a gesture towards slimming during their stay.

A brainwave struck her. 'Oh yes, I know I'm meant to be on the same diet, but I forgot to mention my *allergy*.'

The word had the desired effect; a cowed look of respect appeared in the waitress's eye. 'Ah, Dr Potter usually deals with allergies, but I'm afraid he's not in this evening.'

'Then I'd better see Mr Arkwright.' Without sacrificing any of its charm, Mrs Pargeter's voice allowed no possibility of denial.

She rose to her feet. 'If you'll excuse me, Kim . . . I'll have to just go and sort this out.'

'Yes, of course.'

The waitress looked dubiously down at Mrs Pargeter's plate. 'Not quite sure what I should do about this, though.'

She was rewarded by a sweet smile. 'Well, my friend's helping isn't very large. I'm sure she could manage mine too.'

The waitress's expression left no doubt that Mrs Pargeter had found the quickest route to blasphemy at Brotherton Hall.

'So, about this allergy, Mrs Pargeter . . ?' said Mr Arkwright, seated in the comfort of his flat on the top floor of Brotherton Hall's East Wing.

'Well, cottage cheese is the main thing, really . . .' she confided, 'but this does sort of affect other things . . .'

'Like?'

'Well, for example, I find that I'm allergic

16

to salad on its own.'

'Oh?'

'You know, when it hasn't got any meat with it.'

'Ah?'

'And in fact I'm very nearly allergic to salad with meat. Certainly cold meat. I'm much less allergic to hot meat with lots of nice hot vegetables and then, if there has to be salad . . . well, if it's just a kind of garnish, I'm not so allergic to that.'

Mr Arkwright made a considerable business of writing some notes down on a clipboard. 'We'll certainly bear that in mind, Mrs Pargeter, in devising the optimum diet for your condition. Anything else we should watch on the allergy front?'

'Well, I find I'm quite allergic to not having three good big meals a day. And I'm totally allergic to not having any wine with my dinner.'

'You have a bad reaction to that?'

'Bad? Oh, I'll say! Positively life-threatening.'

'Hm . . .' Mr Arkwright looked long and thoughtfully at the pad in front of him, but his musings were interrupted by a knock on the door of his dining-room. 'Come in.'

A squat man in waiter's uniform, who looked to be as wide as he was tall, entered carrying a tray whose contents were hidden by silver domes and crisp napkins. Mrs Pargeter smiled at him, but he seemed pointedly to avoid her eye.

'Thank you, Stan. If you could put it down and prepare Mrs Pargeter's medication . . .'

The waiter complied and, when the preparation was complete, handed Mrs Pargeter a glass.

She took it cautiously. 'Is it meant to bubble like that?'

Ankle-Deep Arkwright grinned, unable to maintain the charade any longer. 'Dom Perignon usually does. And don't worry, we've got a nice claret to go with the steak.' He raised his glass. 'Cheers, Mrs P. Great to see you.'

Chapter Three

'Mm, delicious,' said Mrs Pargeter, as she scooped up the last of the cream that had deluged her *crème brûlée*. 'Just delicious.'

'Well, you'll have made Gaston's night,' said Ankle-Deep Arkwright.

'Gaston?'

'Chef. He gets so pissed off with what he usually has to do here — you know, lettuce *au* cottage cheese, cottage cheese *au* lettuce, lettuce *au* lettuce, cottage cheese *au* cottage cheese, all that stuff. Order for a proper meal and he's in seventh heaven. 'Cause he's the real business, you know — trained in Switzerland, ran a restaurant in Covent Garden, done the lot.'

'So why's he here?'

' 'Cause I asked him to come here. Looks good on the brochure — "meals individually prepared by our internationally known chef, Gaston Lenoir". Lot of the snootier old biddies go for that.'

'Even though they're only going to have him "individually preparing" cottage cheese for them?'

19

'Yeah. Daft, isn't it? None of them seem to think that one through. But you got to be up with what the other health spas are offering. Always keep your ear to the ground in this business. You know, if you hear another health spa's doing Saragossa Seaweed Massage, you got to do Saragossa Seaweed Massage. If they're offering Dead Sea Mud Baths, you got to offer Dead Sea Mud Baths.'

'And do you actually offer Dead Sea Mud Baths?'

'You bet. Very effective. One of our most popular treatments. Straighten out your Dead Sea Scrolls for you in no time, madam!'

It came back to Mrs Pargeter that amongst the varied stages of Ankle-Deep Arkwright's career had been a spell as a stand-up comic. She accorded his little joke a little smile, which seemed to relieve him. 'Going back to Gaston, though, "Ank" ' — she deliberately used the diminutive that the late Mr Pargeter had coined — 'has he always been a chef?'

'No, he used to be an accountant and . . . Hey, just a minute . . .' Recollection dawned. 'You *know* him, Mrs P.'

'Really?'

'Yeah. He worked with Mr Pargeter. He done the budgeting side on *Milton Keynes*.' A note of awe came into his voice at the mention of one of the late Mr Pargeter's most spectacular business coups. 'Didn't your old man never mention him to you?'

'Gaston? No, I never heard of anyone called Gaston.'

'No, well, of course he wasn't called Gaston in them days, was he? Called Bennett Wilson, that's his real name — "Nitty" for short. Come on, he done that job in Streatham too . . . you know, that security van. You must remember. The one that went wrong.'

A slight frost had settled on Mrs Pargeter's amiable features. 'My late husband never talked to me about his work. He was always of the opinion that his business life and his home life should be kept well separated.'

'Can see his point. Very sensible that — given the kind of business it was. I mean, it's always the case, isn't it — what your old lady don't know, she can't stand up in court and . . .'

The end of the sentence trickled away as Ankle-Deep Arkwright caught the full blistering beam of Mrs Pargeter's violet eyes. With deliberate tact, he misinterpreted the cause of her displeasure. 'Sorry, don't know what come over me — calling you an "old lady" and that. Very sorry.'

Mrs Pargeter's sudden frost was not only caused by her habitual desire to know as little as possible about her late husband's business

21

affairs (a desire, incidentally, that he had enthusiastically encouraged), but also by the mention of Streatham.

The late Mr Pargeter's involvement with Streatham had not been one of his most successful business enterprises. Indeed the venture had gone so badly wrong that its aftermath had kept him absent from the conjugal home for some three years.

Mrs Pargeter had felt this enforced separation keenly. Partly, this was because of the close and loving relationship which she and her husband shared, which meant that she had missed him rotten. But her pain had been aggravated by the fact that she knew he had been betrayed in Streatham by one of his closest associates.

Though she kept knowledge of her husband's business affairs to a minimum, the conversation of the men he delegated to 'keep an eye on her' during his involuntary absence did not allow her to be completely unaware of what had happened.

The villain had been Julian Embridge, an unsuccessful research chemist whose fortunes had changed remarkably when he had been taken under her husband's ever-philanthropic wing. The late Mr Pargeter found employment for many varied talents in his spreading empire, and at that time had decided (from a purely altruistic love of knowledge and respect for the sciences) that he wished to direct some of his resources towards chemical research into the comparative efficacy of different explosives.

The disaffected Julian Embridge, then currently embarrassed by misplaced suspicions about the disappearance of valuable drugs from the laboratory that employed him, had been delighted to become the recipient of the late Mr Pargeter's patronage. Their relationship blossomed and — a rare occurrence — Embridge was even introduced socially to his employer's beloved wife, Melita.

She had enjoyed the company of this short, chubby, straw-haired chemist, though she had always felt some reservations about his ultimate reliability. Occasionally into his blue eyes came too uncompromising a light of avarice.

But her husband was delighted with the new recruit, and gave him ever-increasing responsibility and prominence in his business organization. If the late Mr Pargeter could have been described as a captain of industry, then Julian Embridge was the nearest he ever came to appointing a lieutenant. The relationship grew closer and closer.

Until Streatham.

The precise details of what happened were

never clear to Mrs Pargeter, but the outcome was not in doubt. Basically, Julian Embridge had confided all of the late Mr Pargeter's punctiliously laid plans to the very authorities from whom they should most religiously have been kept hidden. The result was that at what should have been the climax in Streatham, the happy resolution of all his preparations, the late Mr Pargeter had found himself confronted by those authorities. And the consequence of that unhappy confrontation had been the separation which still so rankled with Mrs Pargeter.

What rankled even more was the knowledge that Julian Embridge had escaped with all of the Streatham profits (a sum well into seven figures) and then, so far as anyone could tell, vanished off the face of the earth.

Mrs Pargeter was not a vengeful person, but she had made a vow that, if ever the opportunity arose, she would arrange a rendezvous between Julian Embridge and justice.

She was so carried away in these painful recollections that it took another subservient 'Sorry' from Ankle-Deep Arkwright to bring her back to the present.

His apology was accepted with a gracious inclination of her head and he went on, 'Yeah, well, old "Nitty" . . . after Milton Keynes, he'd got a little stash and he decided he wanted out of the business. Always desperate to be a chef, apparently, but his parents'd pushed him into accountancy — wanted their son in a job which was "reliable and respectable" . . . which is a bit of a laugh, considering the kind of accountant "Nitty" ended up as.'

Mrs Pargeter greeted this reference to possible wrongdoing with a wrinkled brow of puzzlement. 'So, straight after Milton Keynes, he went to Switzerland and started training?'

' 'Sright. Loved every minute of it — cooking exotic dishes. Always used to say it made a change from cooking the books!'

Mrs Pargeter did not seem particularly amused by this witticism, and Ankle-Deep Arkwright moved quickly on. 'So, anyway, when I set up this gaff, I asked old "Nitty" — or "Gaston" as he was by then — if he'd come in with me. Wasn't keen at first, but, you know, old pals' act, honour among —' He recovered himself just in time. 'Well, you know what I mean . . .'

'And is he the only one of my late husband's associates whose help you've enlisted?'

'Few've been in and out — you know, when other commitments permitted . . . but the only other regular's Stan.'

'Stan who brought the food?'

'Yeah. Didn't you recognize him?' Mrs Pargeter shook her head. 'Used to do a lot of legwork for Mr P. Fixed up everything, and the things — usually people — he couldn't fix up, well, he *stitched* them up, didn't he? That's how he got his nickname.'

'Which is . . ?'

' "Stan the Stapler".'

'Ah.'

'There was other reasons why he got called that, actually. If people was being a bit . . . difficult . . . you know, unwilling to talk and that, Stan used to have this great staple gun that . . .' Once again, Mrs Pargeter's expression decided Ankle-Deep Arkwright against continuing. 'Yeah, well, anyway . . . don't know how I'd manage without Stan. He can do it all.'

Mrs Pargeter decided it would be imprudent to ask precisely what this 'all' comprised. 'He didn't seem particularly friendly towards me when he came in.'

'Oh, don't worry about that. Just his manner. Stan can't talk, you know, never could, something wrong at birth. Makes him, like, a bit shy, awkward with people, know what I mean?'

Mrs Pargeter felt partially reassured. 'Going back to Gaston, though . . .'

' "Nitty", yeah?'

'Does he get many orders like mine tonight?'

Ankle-Deep Arkwright shook his head firmly. 'No way. Very much *verboten* at Brotherton Hall.'

'But I'm sure some of the old biddies'd be happy to pay for decent food.'

'Oh, certainly, but that's not the point. Very competitive, like I said, this health spa business. Real dachshund-eat-dachshund out there it is.'

'Why do you say "dachshund"?'

'Because it's a *low-fat* dog!' Once again the delivery was a reminder of his stand-up days. Ankle-Deep Arkwright chuckled at his witticism before continuing, 'No, but to be serious. Lot of competition. If it got around that women coming to Brotherton Hall was actually' — he shook his head with disapproval before italicizing the phrase — *'having a good time . . .'*

'Yes?'

'Well, that'd be the end, wouldn't it?'

Chapter Four

At the end of their meal, Ankle-Deep Arkwright had opened a venerable and princely Armagnac; for some hours they had indulged in that and further reminiscence. So Mrs Pargeter was a little unsteady as she moved up the staircases and through the corridors of Brotherton Hall to her room on the second floor. (Guests' rooms were all on the first and second floors; the third, marked 'Private', contained staff accommodation.)

In the course of their conversation, Ank and Mrs Pargeter had established some useful ground rules for her stay at the health spa. She was to be accorded 'Special Treatment' for an unspecified medical condition. (Mrs Pargeter had suggested 'gluttony', but Ankle-Deep Arkwright was far too much of a gentleman to go along with that.)

This 'Special Treatment' excused her any form of other treatment that she didn't fancy. It was like a school sick note that would get her off aerobics, exercise bicycling, swimming, weight-training . . . presumably also Saragossa Seaweed Massage and Dead Sea

Mud Baths, if they were prescribed. Any activities she did want to have a go at, she was of course at liberty to indulge in. And any that she did want to do one day but didn't want to the next (or vice versa), she could do or not do as the whim took her.

Her 'Special Treatment' status would be confirmed by the Brotherton Hall resident medic, Dr Potter.

'But won't he make a fuss about it, Ank?' Mrs Pargeter had asked.

'Good heavens, no, Mrs P.!' Ankle-Deep Arkwright had roared with laughter. 'Dr Potter'll sign anything I tell him to.'

Also because of her unspecified medical condition, Mrs Pargeter would not be allowed to eat with the rest of the guests. Instead, her meals would be served in specially prepared 'Allergy Room' (situated conveniently adjacent to Gaston's kitchen). All she would have to do each evening would be to check through the following day's menu and make her selections (bearing in mind that, because of his Swiss training, almost all Gaston's main dishes came accompanied by *rosti,* and that the primary ingredient of all his sweets was cream).

Oh yes, and she'd get a wine list each evening to make her selection from that too.

To Mrs Pargeter this all seemed very satisfactory.

As she swanned dreamily along the corridor to her room, she was surprised to see the adjacent door open and Kim Thurrock's face peer anxiously out. Mrs Pargeter felt a moment's guilt for having so completely forgotten her friend.

'Was it all right?' Kim hissed.

'Was what all right?'

'The allergy, of course.'

'Oh.' Mrs Pargeter recovered herself. 'Yes, I think they've probably got the measure of it.'

'That's a relief.'

'Yes. Sorry I couldn't get back earlier. I hope you haven't been too bored . . .'

'Oh no!' Kim Thurrock's eyes gleamed with excitement. 'I've had a wonderful time. They have lectures every evening, you know. And tonight it was — Sue Fisher!'

'Oh,' said Mrs Pargeter, to whom the name carried less immediate import than it clearly did for her friend. 'Sue Fisher?'

'You know, the one who wrote *Mind Over Fatty Matter*.'

'Oh.' Yes, it did ring a bell now. Indeed, one would have to have been immured as a hermit over the previous two years for the name to set up no tintinnabulation at all. The *Mind Over Fatty Matter* book and its sequels had taken up permanent residence in the bestsellers' lists; the *Mind Over Fatty Matter* television series seemed to be screened daily; the *Mind Over Fatty Matter* videos crowded the shelves of record shops; and one could not walk down a high street in the British Isles without passing a display of *Mind Over Fatty Matter* leotards, leggings, and exercise bras, or enter a food store without seeing *Mind Over Fatty Matter* microwave meals and dietary supplements.

All this had made Sue Fisher, the originator of the *Mind Over Fatty Matter* diet and exercise regime, extremely rich. Like some tropical parasite she had burrowed her way into the national obsession with weight, there to take up residence and feed — though not of course fatten — herself on that collective neurosis.

'Was she interesting?' asked Mrs Pargeter.

'Oh, she was *wonderful!*' The enthusiasm invested in the word made it clear that only the inconvenient organization of shop opening hours had prevented Kim from rushing out already to stock up with books, videos, leotards, leggings, exercise bras, microwave meals and dietary supplements.

Still, the fact that her friend had had a good time made Mrs Pargeter feel less guilty about the contrasting way in which she had enjoyed her own evening. 'Oh, I'm so pleased, Kim,' she said comfortably. 'Well, I must get to bed.'

'Yes, see you in the dining-room for breakfast . . . though I think it's just hot water and lemon the first day.'

'Ah. Well, actually,' said Mrs Pargeter, 'I won't be having my meals in the dining-room.'

'Why ever not?'

'Erm . . .' She prevaricated. 'Something to do with the allergy.'

'Oh?' Alarm sprang into Kim Thurrock's eyes. 'You are going to be all right, Melita — aren't you?'

'Yes,' Mrs Pargeter replied. 'Yes, Kim, I think I'm going to be absolutely fine.'

The alcohol brought deep and dreamless sleep, but also ensured that Mrs Pargeter woke at five o'clock, needing the comforts of her *ensuite* bathroom.

As the flushing of the lavatory gurgled to nothing, she was aware of a slight scraping noise from outside.

She peered through the curtains. It was June and already nearly light. Mrs Pargeter found she was looking down on the ornamental fishponds of the landscaped gardens which were one of Brotherton Hall's chief glories. Just on the edge of her vision, she could see something moving. It appeared to be human, but the angle of the building impeded her view.

Intrigued, and now wide awake, Mrs Pargeter found her curiosity aroused. Surely it was a bit early for gardening . . ?

Then she remembered that at the end of the corridor by the stairs was a large window commanding a view directly over the fish-ponds. Why not? It was worth a look. Donning her Brotherton Hall towelling gown, Mrs Pargeter slipped quietly out of her room and along the corridor.

The window at the end was covered only by a thin net curtain, through which she could clearly see what was going on.

Two wheelbarrows stood by the largest fish-pond and between them was Stan the Stapler with a shovel. The squat figure kept reaching into the pond and dragging out shovelfuls of weed or mud. The weed he slopped into one wheelbarrow, the mud into the other.

It was *possible* that he was gardening, doing some essential maintenance work on the ponds.

It was *possible* that he was engaged in some more sinister activity.

Recovering a cache of drugs?

Attempting to drag the pond for a body?

But Mrs Pargeter had a more prosaic explanation for what was going on. And it was one that would conform well with what she knew of Ankle-Deep Arkwright's business practices. She loved Ank dearly, but would have found it hard to hold him up as a paragon of probity.

No, Mrs Pargeter felt pretty convinced that Stan the Stapler was stocking up with Saragossa Seaweed and Dead Sea Mud.

She was just turning back towards her room when she heard the click of a door opening on the floor above.

It lasted only a few seconds. The door clicked open; a snatch of a woman's voice was heard; the door was softly closed and a key turned in the lock. That was all.

But it was what the woman said that stopped Mrs Pargeter in her tracks and traced a little finger of ice down her spine.

A young woman's voice. A voice full of pain, anguish, and despair.

It had said, 'But there's nothing you can do about it. They're going to kill me, and nobody can stop them.'

Chapter Five

Mrs Pargeter and Kim Thurrock spent the Monday, their first full day at Brotherton Hall, rather differently.

Kim, in common with all the other guests (well, except for Mrs Pargeter) started with the Seven-Thirty Weigh-In. This ceremony — not actually called a 'ceremony', but treated with all the pomp of a coronation — was designed to instil into everyone a proper sense of humility. Harsh reality, spelt out in unarguable pounds and ounces, induced shame and an increased incentive to attain the fantasy of a few pounds or ounces less.

After that sobering experience, Kim Thurrock, fortified by her hot water and lemon breakfast, underwent an hour of aerobics, followed by swimming and weight-training. Her lunch, an exotic *mélange* of cottage cheese and lettuce (garnished with more cottage cheese), preceded a Dead Sea Mud Bath, which set on her like mortar and, if only they could have got it off in one piece, would have made the perfect mould for anyone interested in producing Kim Thurrock clones.

After this she was lashed savagely with Saragossa Seaweed by Lindy Galton. (The Brotherton Hall staff were all qualified to perform all the varied tasks of the health spa, and undertook them in turn, according to some elaborate roster.) Kim then had her pores deep-cleansed with something that in any other environment would have been recognized as a pan-scourer. An hour more aerobics and a very long ride on an exercise bicycle ensured that she was more than ready for her supper, which offered the gastronomic treat of the day — breast of a chicken who had evidently been a recent winner of Brotherton Hall's Slimmer of the Year Contest. This sliver of meat was parsimoniously garnished with, yes, more lettuce, and the whole complemented by a rather soapy mineral water.

Kim's day was then completed by a lecture on *Body-Tautness Through Yoga*, followed by another ugly encounter with the collective conscience of all the guests, the Nine O'Clock Weigh-In. At this ritual those who had put on weight were vilified, those who had kept the same weight were castigated, and those who had lost weight were discouraged from complacency and asked why they hadn't lost more.

This regime ensured that everyone went to bed in a proper state of humble inadequacy, determined to spend even more time and money at Brotherton Hall.

Mrs Pargeter's day was different in almost every particular. After a Full English Breakfast (including Black Pudding), she returned to the 'Allergy Room' for lunch (Salmon Steaks, blissfully garnished with gooseberry sauce and of course *rosti, Charlotte Malakov aux Fraises,* enhanced by a good bottle of Sancerre) and dinner (*Faisan au Vin de Porto,* garnished with prunes and of course *rosti, Meringue Glacé,* a very decent Barolo, and some more of the princely Armagnac). Gaston Lenoir (formerly 'Nitty' Wilson) was simply ecstatic to have someone to show off to.

But Mrs Pargeter did not totally neglect the facilities offered by Brotherton Hall. She read a lot of magazines and dozed in the solarium. She spent a very relaxing time in the jacuzzi and after that had a massage, having first checked firmly that no Saragossa Seaweed (or Brotherton Hall Pondweed) was going to be involved in the process. Her enquiries were rewarded by a deliciously benign pummelling from a large masseur whose initial training had been as a baker.

For both it was a delightful experience. Mrs Pargeter felt herself transported to new heights of physical well-being; while for the masseur the kneading of her warm, abundant, scented flesh piquantly brought back the early days of his apprenticeship.

Though Mrs Pargeter and Kim Thurrock spent their days so differently, it would be a hard call to say which one enjoyed herself more.

The one mildly discordant note in Mrs Pargeter's day was struck by her visit to the Brotherton Hall doctor for the medical ratification of her 'Special Treatment' status.

It was not that Dr Potter made any demur about granting her sick-note — his actions were as unimpeded by ethical considerations as Ankle-Deep Arkwright had suggested they would be — it was just that Mrs Pargeter did not care for him very much.

In spite of his fussily dapper suit, the doctor's appearance did not inspire confidence. The thin skin of his face was stretched tight over prominent cheekbones and a surprisingly small nose; it looked completely smooth, but when he grimaced — which is what he did instead of smiling — it broke up into a tracery of tiny parallel lines.

There was something slightly out of true about the set of his eyes, which was accentuated by the deepness of their colour, an indefinable muddy hue like the deep silt of an estuary.

And his hair was obviously dyed, to that over-hearty chestnut which is apparently the only brown available to greying men. Though she had been happy to let her own hair settle to its natural white, Mrs Pargeter had nothing against the principle of hair-colouring, but she thought it looked better on women than men. It was still the case that while women might use hair colour as an exotic fashion accessory, men almost always aspired to a natural look; and it was therefore somehow disappointing when they failed to achieve this effect as totally as Dr Potter had done.

There was also something strange about the man's proportions. He looked short when sitting down; but Mrs Pargeter was surprised how much taller than her he was when he rose to his feet.

Nor was there anything comforting about his manner. Though, given the reason for her visit to his surgery, Mrs Pargeter had not been expecting the full bedside empathy, she had hoped for a little more effort at charm. Being nice to people, however, was evidently low on Dr Potter's priorities. He signed the required documentation for her, but did not waste any energy on smiles or pleasantries.

Mrs Pargeter quickly decided that the appointment of such an unprepossessing doctor was another part of Ankle-Deep Arkwright's marketing strategy. The proprietor knew that his guests came to Brotherton Hall primarily to fuel the hatred they felt for their bodies. Surrounding them with perfectly proportioned female staff and offering the services of an unsympathetic medical adviser could only help in their process of willing self-abasement.

Also on that first day, Mrs Pargeter met the 'wonderful' Sue Fisher. Whom she found almost as unappealing as Dr Potter.

The goddess of *Mind Over Fatty Matter* had not come to Brotherton Hall solely to deliver her lecture of the previous evening. She had done that simply because she was there and could not resist the prospect of motivating yet more sales of *Mind Over Fatty Matter* products.

The real reason for her presence was that Brotherton Hall had received the inestimable honour of featuring as background to her latest *Mind Over Fatty Matter* video.

How much bargaining had preceded this arrangement, and what kind of deal Ankle-Deep Arkwright had eventually struck to attain it could not be known, but there was no doubt that the negotiations had been tough. The secret of Sue Fisher's success lay not in her invention of the *Mind Over Fatty Matter* regime, but in her skilful promotion and marketing of it. She was fully aware of the value of a casual camera panning across the name of any health spa on one of her videos, and had undoubtedly ensured that Brotherton Hall paid appropriately — or, more likely, excessively — for the privilege.

But the way she queened it over the filming showed she had no doubt of who was the senior partner in any deal with Ankle-Deep Arkwright. Just as her regime had eliminated every milligram of unnecessary fat from her body, so she had excluded from her conversation all unnecessary words — like 'please' and 'thank you'.

But this did not seem to diminish her standing in the eyes of the infatuated Brotherton Hall guests, who watched the making of the video as if they had ringside seats at the Second Coming.

Mrs Pargeter only witnessed a little of the action, as she passed the gym on her way from the 'Allergy Room' to the solarium for an after-lunch doze. The space was full of perfectly formed women, dressed in identical *Mind Over Fatty Matter* leotards, leggings, and, presumably, exercise bras. The participants had been shipped in for the occasion; the suggestion, tentatively offered at question-time after her lecture of the previous night, that Sue Fisher might include some of the current Brotherton Hall guests in her video, had been slapped down with instant and humiliating contempt.

In the middle of these perfect fat-free bodies was the most perfect of the lot, the one that belonged to Sue Fisher herself. When casting for her videos she followed the bridesmaid selection process of a canny bride, and always chose bodies which, though they looked perfect by average standards, were fractionally inferior to her own. This, and the contrastingly vivid design of her own *Mind Over Fatty Matter* leotard, leggings, and exercise bra, left no doubt where the focus of attention should be.

As Mrs Pargeter passed, the goddess was taking the other bodies — and from the way she treated them that was patently how she thought of them — through their paces in an aerobic routine. Though they had been schooled to the precision of a Broadway chorus line, Sue Fisher could still find grounds for criticism on every run. She singled out individuals in the line-up with great spite and relish; she bawled out the cameraman, the lighting man, the PA, Ankle-Deep Arkwright, and anyone else who got within her range.

And yet no one answered her back. No one was even mildly perturbed by her spoilt-child behaviour. And the health spa guests seemed to feel especially blessed to be allowed to witness it.

Mrs Pargeter reflected, not for the first time, that there is within the human psyche an infinite yearning for humiliation. Without which, of course, there would be no call for places like Brotherton Hall — and no television game shows either.

That particular yearning, however, had no place in Mrs Pargeter's psyche, so she did not linger to watch more of Sue Fisher's bad manners. She moved on to the solarium to enjoy the next stage of her nice day.

And it really was a nice day, a day whose tranquillity was only occasionally ruffled by the recollection of the anguished young woman's voice Mrs Pargeter had heard at five o'clock that morning.

Chapter Six

The niceness of her day ended at ten past nine in the evening. At that time all of the other guests were locked into the obsessive self-recrimination of the Nine O'Clock Weigh-In. Mrs Pargeter was the only one at liberty on the corridors of Brotherton Hall, floating peaceably along, full of *Faisan au Vin de Porto* and *Meringue Glacé* and Barolo and Armagnac.

So she was the only one to see two burly uniformed ambulance men wheeling a trolley out of a room on the third floor.

Mrs Pargeter was just coming up the stairs to the second landing and caught a glimpse of the men above through the struts of the banisters. She froze while they negotiated the trolley through the door.

One ambulance man stopped and looked round. 'Be easier to get her down if there was a lift,' he growled. 'You notice a lift?'

His colleague shook his head and gestured down the corridor. 'Be along that way if there is one. Let's have a butcher's.'

They both started off, moving away from

44

the stairs. Then the first one was stopped by a sudden thought. 'Should we just leave the trolley here?'

'Not going to make a lot of difference to *her*, is it?'

'I don't mean that. Suppose someone saw her or . . ?'

'We still got twenty minutes. Said so long as we get her out and on the way by nine-thirty, we'd have no problems.'

Reassured, the two ambulance men turned the corner of the corridor and moved out of sight.

Mrs Pargeter, the fumes of Barolo and Armagnac instantly flushed out of her brain, hurried up the last two stairs and approached the trolley.

The body was covered by a sheet. After a quick glance to check for the ambulance men, Mrs Pargeter flicked it back.

At first sight, she thought she saw a child's face, but closer inspection showed it to be older. A girl in her late teens, early twenties, it was hard to say. The hair was so patchy and uneven on the scalp.

And the face was so thin. So very thin, its skin waxy and white, stretched over the bones like greaseproof paper.

The deep-socketed eyes were open, frozen in an expression of terror.

And a hand, fleshless as a chicken's foot, reached up to the neck, as if still trying to ward off some horrifying assailant.

The girl was undoubtedly dead.

But so thin. So horribly thin.

Chapter Seven

'Anorexia,' said Ankle-Deep Arkwright. 'Anorexia nervosa.' Mrs Pargeter made no response, so he went on, 'It's an illness when adolescent girls deliberately stop eating and —'

'I *know* what it is.'

'Yeah. Well, that's what the hospital says it was. It's quite common, apparently.'

'Not common for people actually to die of it.'

'Happens.'

He shrugged. She could sense he was ill at ease. He kept getting up and moving round his little office behind the main Reception at Brotherton Hall, and his eyes wouldn't meet hers.

Also he'd tried to get out of the meeting. She'd searched him out before breakfast on the Tuesday morning and asked about the body, but he'd been evasive. Pleading pressures of other business, he'd said he couldn't talk about it then; but if she came to his office at half-past eleven, he'd be free for a short while.

This was unlike the Ankle-Deep Arkwright Mrs Pargeter remembered — indeed, it was unlike the Ankle-Deep Arkwright she had seen up until that moment at Brotherton Hall. His outgoing helpfulness had vanished; he seemed shifty, preoccupied, almost afraid.

'Look, Ank . . .' she'd said, always believing in the direct approach, 'is there something funny going on here?'

He'd jumped like a cat attacked by a water-pistol. 'Funny? No, why should there be? I'm just busy, that's all. Look, we'll talk at half-past eleven. Everything be a lot clearer then.'

Though whether everything would be a lot clearer for her or for him, Ankle-Deep Arkwright didn't say.

Now that the eleven-thirty meeting had arrived, however, he didn't seem any more relaxed or forthcoming.

'But, Ank,' Mrs Pargeter persisted, 'why on earth didn't Dr Potter spot what was wrong with the girl?'

' 'Cause he didn't see her till after she was dead. Then of course he knew what was wrong instantly. Said he knew the hospital would come up with the same diagnosis.'

'So did Dr Potter sign the death certificate?'

'No. He said it would be more ethical for the hospital to do that.'

Why this sudden concern with ethics, Mrs

48

Pargeter wondered, as Ankle-Deep Arkwright went on, 'Look, the kid only arrived yesterday. She would have weighed in and that this morning; then obviously someone would've seen there was something wrong and called Dr Potter. She just didn't give us the chance.'

'But why was she allowed to check in in that condition?'

'We didn't know she was in that condition!' Ankle-Deep Arkwright replied testily. 'Look, someone makes a reservation on the phone, you accept it in good faith. You don't say, "Oh, by the way, you aren't by any chance about to die of anorexia nervosa, are you?" You just don't do that, do you, Mrs P.?' he concluded on a note of pleading.

She wasn't about to let him off the hook that easily. 'Surely whoever checked her in at Reception must've thought she looked odd?'

He gave another of his shifty shrugs. 'If a girl arrives in a big baggy coat, and she's got a hat on so you can't see her hair's falling out . . . come on, who's to notice? It's not our business to be nosy.' His voice took on a note of piety. 'Here at Brotherton Hall we pride ourselves on respecting our guests' privacy, you know.'

Mrs Pargeter snorted. 'There's a difference between respecting your guests' privacy and letting them die for lack of medical attention.'

He was angry now. 'Look, I told you — the girl only arrived yesterday!'

'Are you sure about that?' Mrs Pargeter asked gently. She could not remove from her memory the words she had heard at five o'clock the previous morning; nor could she help feeling they were linked to the girl's death.

'Of course I'm bloody sure!'

'So who checked her in yesterday?'

He was momentarily confused. 'Well, I can't remember who was on duty . . . There are rosters and things that we could have a look at . . . Oh, just a minute, though . . . Yes, it was Lindy Galton. Lindy Galton was on Reception four to eight yesterday afternoon.'

'Oh well, I could check it out with her then,' said Mrs Pargeter casually.

'You could, yes. But not today. Lindy's day off.'

'That's a pity . . .'

'Yes.' But he didn't seem to think it was as much of a pity as she did.

'. . . because Kim and me're off tomorrow.'

He shrugged in satisfied helplessness, then changed tack and tried an appeal for sympathy. 'Look, you must realize, Mrs P., that this, er . . . *incident* is extremely embarrassing. I mean, particularly embarrassing given the nature of the business I'm running here. A death from anorexia at a health spa — just think what kind of a meal the tabloids could make of that one.'

Mrs Pargeter did not give an inch, and stayed silent.

'Surprising, I suppose, that it doesn't happen more often,' Ankle-Deep Arkwright floundered on. 'Presumably for an anorexic girl, there is a kind of logic about it. You're obsessed with losing weight, so you book into a health spa to lose more.'

'I'm not sure that that's how it'd work. Anorexics rarely draw attention to their condition. It's something very private for them, something whose existence a lot of them won't even admit.'

'Well . . . , Well . . .' He looked lost. 'Clearly in this case the girl's mind worked differently. Listen, Mrs P.' — pleading had now been replaced by begging — 'it's very important that we keep what's happened to ourselves. I mean, it could be absolutely disastrous for business if —'

Mrs Pargeter cut through all this. 'What's the girl's name?'

'Jenny Hargreaves. Well, that was the name on the things I found in her room. I went up there this morning to check the place out.'

He hastily remembered something else. 'And Jenny Hargreaves was of course what she registered under, so I can only assume it was her real name.'

'You're positive it was only yesterday that she did register?'

'Of course I am! Really, Mrs P. — don't you trust me or something?' He thought better of giving her time to answer the question. 'I can show you the records. Our registration system is all computerized.'

He went through to the reception area and returned almost immediately with a couple of sheets torn off a computer print-out. These he thrust towards her. 'Look, Mrs P., there you are — Jenny Hargreaves checked in at six-forty yesterday evening.'

The details were undeniably printed out. 'Why is the credit-card reference blank?' asked Mrs Pargeter.

There was an infinitesimal pause before Ankle-Deep Arkwright replied, 'Not everyone pays by credit card. We accept cheques — or even old-fashioned cash,' he added with an unsuccessful attempt at humour.

'Hmm . . .' Mrs Pargeter still looked at the print-out in front of her. 'Her address is a college in Cambridge.'

'So . . ?'

'I'd've thought Brotherton Hall was rather

52

an expensive place for a student, wouldn't you?'

Once again, Ankle-Deep Arkwright just shrugged.

'Mason de Vere Detective Agency.'

The voice was terminally lugubrious and immediately recognizable.

'Truffler. It's Mrs Pargeter.'

'Oh, how wonderful to hear you,' he said, in the tones of a man who'd just received a ransom demand for his favourite and only daughter. Truffler Mason's manner had been gloomy back in his days of working for the late Mr Pargeter, and when, following his beloved boss's death, he moved into a more publicly acceptable area of private investigation, the gloom had gone with him.

'What's with all this answering your own phone, Truffler? Haven't you got any staff?'

'Had to let them go. There is a recession on, you know,' Truffler Mason replied, sounding a little more cheerful now he had something genuinely depressing to talk about.

'Enough of a recession for you to have time to do a little investigation for me, Truffler?'

'Doesn't need to be a recession for that, Mrs Pargeter. Recession, boom-time, any time, you know you have only to ask. Anything.

Honestly, when I think of all the things the late Mr Pargeter done for me —'

'Yes, yes. I do appreciate your saying that, Truffler . . .' And she did. It was just that she had heard it so many times before.

'So what is it then?' he asked, suddenly businesslike. 'You haven't got yourself involved in another murder, have you, Mrs Pargeter?'

'No. Well, at least I'm fairly sure I haven't. I have got myself involved in an unexplained death, though.'

'Where are you calling from?'

'Brotherton Hall, don't know if you know the place. It's a health spa.'

'Oh? Unexplained death at a health spa . . . I say, that sounds as if someone's been *wasted*,' he said from the even deeper gloom which signified that he was telling a joke.

'You don't know how horribly near the truth you are, Truffler.'

Putting the inadvertent lapse of taste behind him, he hastily asked, 'So what can I do for you?'

'I want you to find out everything you can about the dead girl. Her name was Jenny Hargreaves, she was apparently a student at Cambridge University, and there seems little doubt she died of anorexia nervosa.'

'Oh,' said Truffler Mason.

'I've got a college address for her, but that's

all. Be enough for you to get started, will it?'

'Mrs Pargeter, I'm offended you had to ask.'

But Truffler Mason's voice didn't sound offended. Instead it was weighed down with that extra despondency which signified his excitement at the beginning of a new investigation.

Chapter Eight

For lunch that day Mrs Pargeter enjoyed a *Brochette de Lotte* and *Mousse aux Deux Chocolats* in a meaningfully symbiotic relationship with an excellent Muscadet (the new coolness between herself and Ankle-Deep Arkwright had not affected Gaston's dedication to the challenge of impressing her), and then set out to find Kim. She needed to ascertain whether any of the other guests had been aware of the departure of a corpse from Brotherton Hall the previous evening.

Her search ended in the gym, which, having been cleared of guests for the making of the *Mind Over Fatty Matter* video, was now full of less perfect bodies, losing the unequal struggle against weight-training apparatus, walking machines, and exercise bicycles.

Kim was busting a gut on a rowing machine. Marketing had done its work and she was now wearing *Mind Over Fatty Matter* leotards, leggings, and exercise bra. Somehow they didn't look as good on her as they had on Sue Fisher's aerobic chorus-line.

It was dreadful to see the agonies Kim was

going through, scrunching her body up on each forward push and straining as the sliding seat clacked along beneath her with each pull back. Mrs Pargeter could not imagine anything more uncomfortable, and indeed could not imagine a human mind voluntarily consenting to such torture.

But Kim's sweat-streaked face gleamed with pleasure. In fact it was more than pleasure; her expression showed the fervour of the postulant, the convert brought to ecstasy by the mysteries of her new religion. Brotherton Hall was certainly doing what was required of it for Kim Thurrock.

Mrs Pargeter parked herself on the seat of an adjacent exercise bicycle. 'How're you doing, love?' she asked.

'Wonderful,' Kim gasped through her torments. 'You really ought to have a go.'

Mrs Pargeter demurred with a little shake of her head.

'No, it needn't be something as vigorous as this. They've got apparatus that's much gentler. Look, those things over there are called passive exercisers. You just lie down on them and they do the exercising for you.'

Kim nodded towards a pair of machines rather like loungers, whose arm and leg supports rose and fell rhythmically to stretch the limbs of the women who lay on them.

'Those're dead easy, Melita. The machine does the work for you. You could have a go on that, couldn't you?'

Though admittedly not as daunting as the other apparatus, the passive exercisers were still not for Mrs Pargeter. 'Don't think it'd be wise. You know, the allergy . . .'

The magic word elicited the usual subdued reaction. Mrs Pargeter, to show she wasn't going to let her allergic condition get her down, smiled pluckily. 'Anyway, Kim, how's it really going for you?'

'Marvellous! Do you know, I'd lost four ounces at the Seven-Thirty Weigh-In this morning.'

'Oh, well done.'

'Thicko won't recognize me.'

'I'm sure he will. After all, he's seen you at Visiting every week for nearly seven years.'

'Yes, I know. I mean, he won't recognize me when . . . well, you know, bed . . .' A blush struggled through to intensify the sweaty redness of her face. 'Anyway, I'm going to have my hair done differently before I leave here.'

'How're you going to have it done?' Kim's natural frizzy blonde hair, currently scraped back under a drenched sweat-band, had always struck Mrs Pargeter as one of her friend's chief glories.

'Well, probably red. Thicko always had a thing about redheads.'

'Thicko always had a thing about *you*,' Mrs Pargeter chided. 'Don't you go changing yourself too much. You don't want your hair coloured, Kim. You're much better off with what's natural.'

'Oh, but this would be natural. The Brotherton Hall salon only uses *Mind Over Fatty Matter* hair preparations' (Dear God, was there any area of consumerism that Sue Fisher hadn't got into?) 'and they're all natural products. I've bought a lot of them already.' (Yes, I bet you have.) 'You know, they're made from herbs and barks of trees and mineral deposits and all that. And, what's more,' Kim added piously, 'none of them have been tested on animals.'

'Well, I'd keep them away from the poodles when you get home.'

'Why?'

'Because they'll probably kill them.'

But Kim Thurrock was too excited by her fitness programme to react to — or even to recognize — jokes. 'Another thing I was thinking of having done — not immediately, but maybe in a little while — is a nip and tuck.'

'Sorry?'

'You know, only a little bit. Empty the bags

under the eyes, pick up the bottom a tidge.'

'Are you talking about plastic surgery, Kim?' asked Mrs Pargeter, appalled.

'Of course I am. A lot of the other guests've had it done. One of them was telling me Mr Arkwright knows a very good plastic surgeon.'

Mrs Pargeter recalled that Ankle-Deep Arkwright had also known 'a very good plastic surgeon' in his former career. But that character, known universally as 'Jack the Knife' had employed his skills in rather specialized areas. He had made a fresh start possible for a great many people whose career prospects would otherwise have been blighted. Indeed the fact that Lord Lucan continued to work without harassment as a publican in Docking was a tribute to the expertise of Jack the Knife.

But it was no time for reminiscence. Rather sharply, Mrs Pargeter said, 'You just keep away from plastic surgery, Kim. You're fine as you are.'

'But I'm *not*. That's the whole point.'

'Listen, my girl —'

Kim Thurrock was not in the mood for a lecture. 'Never mind that. Just tell me — how's Brotherton Hall going for you, Melita?' she asked, straining once again to fold her body in half.

'Oh, fine, thanks.'

'Enjoying all the facilities?'

'Well, yes. At least,' she conceded righteously, 'those my "Special Treatment" allows me to.'

'It is rotten luck for you,' Kim puffed, 'being kept off the gym equipment.'

'Heart-breaking,' Mrs Pargeter agreed demurely.

'And I hope the food you get in that "Allergy Room" isn't too ghastly.'

Mrs Pargeter conceded bravely that it was just about tolerable.

'Do you know, Melita — I was offered a quarter of a grapefruit this morning at breakfast . . .'

'Lucky you.'

'But of course I refused it.'

'Why?'

'Well, it's terribly easy to get complacent. You know, when you're feeling all good about having lost four ounces, well, that's just the time you're in danger of going on a binge.'

Mrs Pargeter was about to question whether eating a quarter of a grapefruit constituted 'going on a binge', but there didn't really seem much point. She knew that the vigour of Kim's new faith would be resistant to all such heresies. So instead she asked, 'You didn't hear any rumours of anything odd happening yesterday evening, did you, Kim?'

'Odd?'

'Yes, odd, like . . .' She wasn't sure how to continue. She didn't want to say 'odd like a dead body being wheeled out on a trolley'. Nor did she wish to refer to the sight she had seen from the second-floor window of the same body being loaded into an ambulance by the two ambulance men and Stan the Stapler. 'Just odd like someone being ill or something . . ?' she concluded lamely.

'No. Nothing odd like that,' Kim replied between grunts. 'Good heavens, you can't imagine anything unpleasant happening to anyone at Brotherton Hall, can you?'

But Mrs Pargeter could, all too easily.

Chapter Nine

She decided to go back to the solarium, where she was planning to snooze out the afternoon, via Reception. Although Ankle-Deep Arkwright had said it was Lindy Galton's day off, he might have been lying, and there was a long chance that the girl would once again be on reception duty.

As it turned out, there was no one behind the counter in the foyer. That was not unusual. Brotherton Hall had two busy times for registration. Day guests arrived before ten, and most of those who were staying longer would check in between four and six, in time for the delights of their first cottage cheese evening meal. For the rest of the day, whoever was on reception duty was often busy elsewhere, returning to the foyer at a summons from the bell-push on the counter.

Mrs Pargeter didn't press the bell-push. Her business at Reception could be more easily accomplished without the help of a receptionist. Turning to check that there was no one watching, she slipped behind the counter.

In spite of everything Ankle-Deep Arkwright had said, she was still convinced of a link between the body removed the previous night and the anguished voice she had heard the morning before. For there to be no connection was too much of a coincidence.

The most likely scenario was that the voice had belonged to the dead girl, her prophecy 'They're going to kill me, and nobody can stop them' having been horribly fulfilled.

But who 'they' were, and how 'they' were going to kill her, were questions to whose answers Mrs Pargeter had, without further research, no clues at all.

There were other questions, though, to which she might be able to find answers. Like whether Jenny Hargreaves' registration details had been tampered with.

Because if it had been the dead girl whom Mrs Pargeter had heard speaking on the last morning of her life, then she had certainly checked in to Brotherton Hall before six-forty the previous evening, the time to which Ankle-Deep Arkwright had testified.

But computer records could easily be amended. Now she came to think of it, Mrs Pargeter was struck by the ease with which Ank had found the relevant piece of print-out.

Almost as if he had been waiting to be asked for it.

Mrs Pargeter didn't know much about computers, but nor apparently did the reception staff at Brotherton Hall. Just in front of the keyboard, out of sight to the registering guests, a typewritten idiot's guide to the system had been Sellotaped on to the counter.

The relevant section of these instructions read:

PRESS 'G' FOR FULL GUEST LIST. MOVE CURSOR TO NAME AND PRESS 'RETURN' TO BRING INDI-VIDUAL DETAILS UP ON SCREEN. FOR NEW ARRIVALS, PRESS 'R' TO BRING BLANK REGISTRATION FORM UP ON SCREEN.

Even a computer illiterate like Mrs Pargeter could cope with that. A single press of the 'G' key filled the screen with surnames, listed alphabetically. After a couple of false attempts she found the key which controlled the cursor and moved it down the left-hand side of the screen.

There was no name between 'HADLEIGH' and 'HARRIS'.

So far as the Brotherton Hall computer was concerned, Jenny Hargreaves had never ex-isted.

Mrs Pargeter was about to press 'R' to bring

on to the screen a blank registration form —
or maybe a registration form with Jenny
Hargreaves' details hastily keyed in — when
she heard the click of Ankle-Deep Arkwright's office door opening behind her and
the sound of angry voices.

She abandoned the computer and moved to
occupy a low armchair behind a pot of tall
ferns, with an agility surprising for a woman
in her late sixties.

She heard Ank's voice first, aggrieved and
whining; it was the voice of a man who knew
he was losing the argument.

'That's unfair! We had a deal!'

The voice that answered was equally sure
that its owner was winning the argument. It
was a voice over which no shadow of doubt
had ever dared to cast itself.

'There are so many ways in which you've
failed to fulfil your side of the deal that it's
hardly worth discussing, Mr Arkwright!'

It was the voice to whose televised and
videoed commands millions of housewives
punished their bodies daily: the voice of Sue
Fisher.

'But, Sue —'

'*Ms Fisher* to you.'

'All right then, *Ms Fisher*, you definitely
agreed that the Brotherton Hall logo would
be featured on your video.'

'That was when you definitely agreed to continue to assist in marketing *Mind Over Fatty Matter* products —'

'I'm not arguing about that. We're quite happy to —'

'Which agreement *includes*,' Sue Fisher continued inexorably, 'trying out such new products as my marketing department chooses to send to you.'

'Well, that's where there is a problem. Nothing against the idea in principle . . . as you know, I've been happy to go along with it in the past. It's just that . . . at the moment there are special circumstances. I think we should lay off the testing for a few —'

'It is not *testing*, Mr Arkwright, it is *trying out!*'

'Maybe, but I'm —'

'Anyway, if you've suddenly gone off testing, perhaps you've also gone off the idea of our marketing your home-pack Brotherton Hall Dead Sea Mud treatment?'

'No, no, obviously I'm still very keen on that.' Ank's voice was now plaintively conciliatory. 'And the moment you want to try out one of our Dead Sea Mud Baths, Ms Fisher, you have only to —'

'Shut up, Mr Arkwright!'

From Mrs Pargeter's fern-screened perspective Sue Fisher's next words sounded louder. She was evidently making a dramatic exit from the office.

'The video we shot here is being edited next week. Starting Monday. If I don't hear from you before then, agreeing to my terms *exactly as I have spelled them out,* I guarantee that I will cut out every shot of the Brotherton Hall logo, every exterior of the house, in fact every clue that might possibly identify your tin-pot premises as the location where the shooting took place! Have you got that, Mr Arkwright?'

This last line came from further off, as Sue Fisher's tall and splendidly tuned body stalked off up the stairs, confident as ever of its owner's unassailable rightness.

Ankle-Deep Arkwright took out his frustration on the computer. 'Bloody girl's left the registration list up,' he murmured savagely, before stabbing at a key and stumping back into his office.

Mrs Pargeter had found the exchange very interesting. For a start, it set a few hares of potential motivation running through her head.

But, perhaps more importantly, it also told her the High Priestess of *Mind Over Fatty Matter* was still at Brotherton Hall. And had presumably been there the previous evening.

Sue Fisher wouldn't have been present at

the Nine O'Clock Weigh-In of the guests for whom she felt such obvious contempt.

Which meant that, like Mrs Pargeter, she too might have witnessed the removal of a corpse from Brotherton Hall.

Assuming, of course, that she didn't have any other involvement in Jenny Hargreaves' death.

Chapter Ten

The red light on the telephone was blinking when Mrs Pargeter got back to her room. She rang through to the switchboard and received the message that a Mr Mason had called.

'Truffler,' she said, as soon as she got through.

'Ah, Mrs Pargeter,' he responded in mournful delight. 'Thank you for getting back so promptly.'

'So . . . have you managed to find some information on Jenny Hargreaves?'

'Just a few starting points,' he replied modestly. 'Nineteen years old. Only child. Brought up in Portsmouth — parents pretty hard-up. Jenny did well at the local comprehensive — one of the few to make it from there through to university. In her second year at Cambridge, studying French and Spanish. Doing very well, good grades and that, until end of last term when she suddenly left a week early. This term's only just started, but there's been no sign of her.'

Not surprising if she's dead, thought Mrs

Pargeter. 'As always, Truffler, your "starting points" are better than most investigators' final reports. Found out anything about her parents?'

'Of course.' He was a little aggrieved that she'd felt the need to ask the question. 'Nice couple. Both retired, must've been quite old when Jenny was born. Living on the state pension — no spare cash for anything.'

'So Jenny'd be on a full grant at Cambridge?'

'Guess so. Not, from all accounts,' he added lugubriously, 'that that goes far these days.'

'No. Boyfriends — anything in that line?'

'Apparently, yes. Tom O'Brien — same year at Cambridge, also doing French and Spanish, though at a different college. Came from a comprehensive too. From all accounts it's a good relationship, love's young dream — though apparently she didn't even tell him where she was going off to at the end of last term.'

'But why didn't someone raise the alarm about her then? Surely when a nineteen-year-old girl just vanishes off the face of the earth someone's going to —'

'Ah, but she didn't just vanish off the face of the earth. Kept ringing her parents through the holidays, every week, telling them she was OK.'

'Did she say where she was or what she was up to?'

'Doing a holiday job, she said. Implied it was market research, interviewing people, that kind of stuff. Didn't say where, though.'

'And the boyfriend — Tom — she didn't call him?'

'Seems not. Jenny only contacted her parents.'

'And Tom didn't check things out with them?'

'Once. Otherwise no. Seems there wasn't that much warmth between Tom O'Brien and the elder Hargreaves.'

'They didn't approve of him?'

'Gather not. From all accounts he's a bit political for their taste.'

'What kind of political? Anarchist bomb-throwing or just youthful idealism?'

'Youthful idealism. Saving the planet, exposing the corporate destroyers of our natural heritage, you know the kind of number. Left-wing with it, though, and it seems that's the bit the Hargreaves couldn't cope with. They're deep-dyed Conservative — you know, as blue as only the respectable and impoverished working class can be.'

'Ah. Have you actually talked to Tom O'Brien, Truffler?'

'No. Most of this stuff I got second-hand.

'Cause that's the funny thing, see . . . Tom hasn't turned up for the beginning of this term either.'

'Oh.' A chilling thought came into Mrs Pargeter's mind. 'I hope nothing's happened to him . . .'

'No reason why it should have done.' In any other voice the words would have brought reassurance. As spoken by Truffler Mason they had the reverse effect.

'No. No, one death's quite enough, isn't it?' Mrs Pargeter was silent for a moment. 'Must be dreadful for the poor girl's parents. I mean, to lose an only child at that age — well, at any age, but particularly when she's just setting out on her adult life . . . dreadful. How did they take the news, Truffler?'

'So far as I can discover, Mrs Pargeter, they don't know about it yet.'

'What?' she asked in surprise.

'I mean, it was less than twenty-four hours after the girl's death that I was checking out the parents . . . hospital might not have had time to track them down yet . . .'

'No, perhaps not,' Mrs Pargeter mused.

'If they still don't know when I'm next in touch . . . do you reckon I should tell them?'

'No. No, Truffler. Give it a bit more time.'

* * *

Mrs Pargeter decided that she needed a bit more time, too. When the booking had been made, she and Kim had agreed, in spite of Ankle-Deep Arkwright's assurances that they could stay as long as they wanted to, that three days would be about right. Which meant they were due to leave in the early evening of the following day, the Wednesday.

But those arrangements had been made before Mrs Pargeter had anything at Brotherton Hall to investigate. Now a rather longer stay was in order. Leaving on the Saturday would be about right.

Kim Thurrock, tracked down once again to the gym where she was doing doughty things with dumb-bells, required the minimum of persuasion. She was so revelling in what she regarded as the pampering of her body (though 'punishment' was the word Mrs Pargeter would have used), that the idea of continuing it was infinitely appealing. And no, the girls were no problem, they loved being looked after by her Mum. So did the poodles.

Also, of course, the longer Kim stayed at Brotherton Hall, the less time she would have before Thicko's release for backsliding from her regime — and the less traitorous pounds would have an opportunity to infiltrate themselves back on to her body.

Ankle-Deep Arkwright was less enthusiastic about the extension to their stay when Mrs Pargeter mooted it. The generosity of his initial welcome changed to much whingeing about the availability of rooms and abject reminders that there was a recession on.

She answered the first objection by checking future bookings at Reception, and the second by insisting that she was happy to pay for the extra days.

Ankle-Deep Arkwright, realizing that further opposition would raise more suspicions than it might quell, agreed miserably.

'What's the matter, Ank?' Mrs Pargeter asked gently. 'There's something upsetting you, isn't there?'

She could see he was torn. Ranked on one side stood his loyalty to the widow of the late Mr Pargeter, and the alluring relief of talking to someone about his problems.

On the other side stood fear. Though fear of what or of whom Mrs Pargeter could not begin to guess.

The fear won.

'All right, Mrs P., go ahead, book the extra days. I can't stop you. But I must tell you that I'm just about to get very busy, so I may not be able to give you quite the personal attention I have up till now.'

The message to Mrs Pargeter was clear. You're on your own. Keep your nose out of my business.

Chapter Eleven

Before the interview finished, Mrs Pargeter asked Ankle-Deep Arkwright whether their disagreement would mean the end of her 'Special Treatment' status, and he fell over himself to assure her that she was still welcome to all of the facilities of the 'Allergy Room'. Again, half of him seemed desperate to get rid of her, while the other half still wanted to provide all the cosseting due to the widow of the late Mr Pargeter.

She got the feeling he was not blocking her progress from any personal animus, but because of pressure from a person or persons unknown. Since Mrs Pargeter had always favoured pulling bushes up by the roots rather than beating about them, she again asked directly what his problem was or who was making his life difficult, but she got nothing back. Ankle-Deep Arkwright clammed up and brought their interview to an abrupt conclusion.

There was not a lot more she could do that day on the investigation front. She was waiting for more information from Truffler Mason, and her enquiries at Brotherton Hall could not progress further until Lindy Galton returned to work the following morning.

But Mrs Pargeter was not the sort to let this enforced idleness prey on her spirits. She resigned herself philosophically to a day of indulgence. Her exercise programme incorporated an hour in the jacuzzi and another sweet nostalgia-inducing massage session with the ex-baker. And she continued to warm the cockles of Gaston's heart by the relish with which she despatched his *Truite aux Amandes Style Paysan* complemented by a *Sorbet de Cassis* at lunchtime, and his *Carré d'Agneau Imperiale* followed by *Tira-mi-su* at dinner.

With the former meal she drank a young Vouvray; with the latter a mature Rioja Gran Reserva as thick and rich as arterial blood.

There were worse ways of spending a day.

Tracking down Lindy Galton the following morning proved harder than it should have been. The girl on Reception confirmed that Lindy was back at work, but then became evasively ignorant of precisely which duties she had been allocated. Whether this ignorance was genuine or commanded by Ankle-Deep Arkwright was impossible to know.

Kim Thurrock proved more helpful. So immersed had she become in the life style of

Brotherton Hall that she seemed to know everything that went on there. Kim, whom Mrs Pargeter found on her back in the gym pushing up impossible-looking weights with her feet, said she thought she'd seen Lindy going through to the Dead Sea Mud Bath area.

So Mrs Pargeter went down to the Brotherton Hall basement, but was denied entrance by an officious teenager with the obligatory perfect body. 'Only guests who've actually booked baths are allowed through,' she announced in less than perfect vowels.

There was nothing else for it. Mrs Pargeter returned to Reception and booked herself a Dead Sea Mud Bath for ten o'clock.

Beneath Brotherton Hall was a considerable network of cellars. Part of this had been developed into a well-appointed basement area, which had been through many incarnations since the building's consecration to the religion of health.

Following the passing fads of fitness regimes, it had housed Steam Baths, Ice Baths, Traditional Turkish Baths, Hose Baths, Needle-Sharp Showers, and Electro-Tingle Pools. (These last were introduced for a treatment whereby very mild electric currents were passed through a guest's bathwater. The facility never proved popular and after a couple of rather nasty electrocutions had been re-placed by Stagnant Water Tubs, another fail-ure.)

The basement's current incarnation was certainly its messiest and, Mrs Pargeter sur-mised, wrinkling her nose as she entered the bath area, probably its most malodorous. Maybe the Dead Sea did smell like that, but she couldn't remove from her mind the im-age of Stan the Stapler and his shovel. A fetid flavour of pondwater hung in the air.

The Dead Sea Mud Bath treatment was, like many such regimes, based on a book. In common with all such fitness books, the ar-gument of *New Life From Dead Sea Mud* could be expressed in one sentence — in this case: 'Dead Sea Mud is good for you.'

But, also in common with all such fitness books, this simple thought was backed up by all kinds of pseudo-scientific research and lots of charts and graphs. Dead Sea Mud, it was asserted, contained unrivalled concentrations of natural chemicals. Filtered and purified through the varied strata of clay, marl, soft chalk, sand, and gypsum, were abundant de-posits of sulphide, potassium, magnesium, bromine, chlorine, and sodium chloride. The fact that the Dead Sea was, at four hundred metres below sea level, the lowest terrestrial area of water, meant that it was closer to the health-giving radiances and healing magnetism of the Earth's core. The mud's anti-corruptive powers had been proved historically because the Dead Sea was reputed to have engulfed the cities of Sodom and Gomorrah. Its mystical significance could be judged from the fact that it was fed by the sacred River Jordon, as well as streams running through the wadis of al-Uzaymi, Zarqa'Ma'in, al-Mawjib, and al-Hasa.

And, needless to say, the book contained some stuff about ley lines.

All of this material had been assembled by a publisher secure in the knowledge that *New Life From Dead Sea Mud* was not the kind of book that anyone would actually read.

Its tiny thesis, supported by some really arty photographs and a couple of meaningless graphs of mineral analysis or weight/body-fat ratios, would be just the right size to fill a colour supplement serialization, which would recoup most of the production costs.

Then the book itself (published in the run-up to Christmas) would be bought by faddists, friends of faddists, husbands trying gently to hint that their wives were letting their appearance go a bit, and women determined to change their lives completely after the breakdown of relationships.

There were sufficient such purchasers about

to ensure reasonable sales figures, or even, with a bit of serendipitous publicity — like, say, a chat-show host showing what a good sport he was by getting into a Dead Sea Mud Bath — an entry into the bestsellers lists.

The fact that none of the purchasers or recipients of the book would read more than a couple of pages did not give the publishers a moment's unease. They felt absolutely confident that they had produced a product with enough confusing words in it to make people think they were learning something. And, more importantly, a product that would sell.

At the end of the process the public consciousness would have assimilated the dubious thesis of the book's title, that 'Dead Sea Mud is good for you'.

And it would stay in the public consciousness until the next fitness fad came along.

The one detail never mentioned anywhere in the book was that any fish foolish enough to stray into the waters of the Dead Sea dies instantly.

Chapter Twelve

The difficulty with mud — whether from the Dead Sea or from the pond of an English stately home — is keeping it muddy. In a centrally heated interior it has a distressing habit of setting, and the mud in the basement of Brotherton Hall needed constant dilution to maintain it at a properly glutinous level.

The Dead Sea Mud Bath unit had, in common with every other facility at the health spa, been installed to a very high specification. Given the costs of that, and the costs of keeping the area spotless, it was no surprise that the Dead Sea Mud Baths were promoted so heavily to the guests. Ankle-Deep Arkwright had to see his installation money back before the arrival of the next fitness fad would require the unit's complete refurbishment.

There were four baths in all, each in a cubicle separated from the others by eight-foot-high walls. The baths themselves were sunken, filled from incongruously gleaming lion's head sluices, and drained by some unseen but presumably very powerful pumping system. Brotherton Hall assured guests that their baths would be individually filled, so that no one had to step into someone else's dirty mud, and presumably that was one of the reasons for the exorbitant costs of the treatment. (Mrs Pargeter's natural cynicism — and knowledge of Ankle-Deep Arkwright's customary business practices — made her pretty sure that some kind of mud-recycling would be going on, but she had no proof of this.)

The lion's heads were fed from a large central tank, in which a stew of mud was kept in constant motion and, it was to be hoped, fluency, by a rotating blade like that used in the mixing of cement or the manufacture of toffee. Because of the viscous nature of its contents, the outlets to this tank frequently became clogged and indeed, when Mrs Pargeter arrived that morning, Stan the Stapler was up on a ladder poking away with a long instrument at some blockage.

By happy coincidence, the other users of the unit were demonstrating the sequence of the treatment.

Through the half-open door of Cubicle One Mrs Pargeter could see a body lying at full length in its tub. So complete was the covering of pale brown sludge (participants were encouraged to smear their faces and work the mud into their hair) that she could not even have told the sex, let alone the identity of the bather. This immersion part of the process was recommended to last for an hour, during which 'the natural salts and minerals can get really deeply into the pores' (Mrs Pargeter shuddered at the very idea).

On a bench outside Cubicle Two, in the glare of a kind of sunlamp, another participant was enjoying the second part of the treatment. This involved letting the mud dry 'naturally' on the skin till it formed a pale beige crust. During this stage guests were encouraged to keep as still as possible, to avoid cracking and flaking. The recommended drying time was also one hour, and again Mrs Pargeter could form no opinion about the identity of the participant — or even whether she had on any underwear.

Cubicle Three was empty, but from it came an abdominal rumbling and gurgling, which presumably denoted that the bath was being drained. On the other side of the unit, the cubicle's most recent occupant was undergoing the most gruelling part of the Dead Sea Mud treatment — getting the bloody stuff off.

Under a ferocious shower a streaked body scrubbed away at itself, directing high-speed jets of water from a hose into its most intimate crevices. Mrs Pargeter had heard from Kim Thurrock that this cleansing process took hours; 'and still at the end of the day when I undressed I found flaky bits in my knickers . . .' The depth of Kim's love affair with everything related to Brotherton Hall can be judged from the fact that she then added fervently, '. . . which *shows* it must've been doing some good.'

Lindy Galton, perfectly proportioned and still immaculately uniformed in spite of the mud that surrounded her, stepped forward to meet her latest client.

'Mrs Pargeter, isn't it?'

'That's right.'

'If you'd like to come through to Cubicle Four, the bath should just about be full now.'

Mrs Pargeter stood inside the doorway, dressed as instructed in only her Brotherton Hall towelling gown over swimwear, and looked down at the contents of the bath as the last strainings plopped in from the lion's head sluice.

The mud could have been said to look like liquid milk chocolate, with a consistency like that of Bolognese sauce — though it has to be confessed that the similes which sprang instinctively to Mrs Pargeter's mind were rather less elegant.

There was a silence as the two of them looked down at the sluggish sludge. 'Well,' Lindy Galton prompted eventually, 'aren't you going to get in?'

'Good heavens, no,' said Mrs Pargeter. 'What on earth do you take me for?'

'Then why are you here?' The girl looked confused rather than alarmed.

Before answering, Mrs Pargeter moved forward to a console of switches on the wall and pressed the one marked 'Empty'. The room was filling with the kind of sounds that can be the consequence of an ill-considered curry.

Lindy Galton stepped towards the console, her face sharp with anger. 'What are you doing? The bath's only just been filled.'

'I'm paying for the Dead Sea Mud Bath treatment,' Mrs Pargeter replied coolly. 'Whether I choose to have it or not I'd have thought was up to me.'

'But why are you emptying it away? Someone else could have the mud.'

'Why, do you want it?' asked Mrs Pargeter, deliberately frivolous.

The reaction — and the distaste — were instinctive. 'No, thank you!'

'Oh, you know where it's come from then, do you?'

The girl seemed about to agree, then remembered her professional role and replied frostily, 'I can't personally go into the mud because of an allergy. I've tried the treatment and I'm afraid it brings me out in a rash.' She gave her client a beady look. 'You still haven't explained why you're emptying the bath.'

'I've started that for the noise . . . so's we can't be overheard,' said Mrs Pargeter in an even whisper.

Now there was a light of alarm in Lindy Galton's eye. 'What is this?'

'I want to ask you about a guest registration you made at Reception a couple of days ago.'

'Oh?'

'A registration for someone called "Jenny Hargreaves".' The girl's eyes told her instantly that she was on to something. 'You see, I think that Jenny Hargreaves arrived at Brotherton Hall earlier than that registration record implies. I think you only keyed those details into the computer because Mr Arkwright told you to.'

Lindy Galton licked a lip that seemed suddenly to have become dry. 'Why do you want to know about this? Why're you interested, Mrs Pargeter?'

'Because I think it could have something to do with a mystery guest at Brotherton Hall. Someone who was staying in a room on the third floor . . . until a couple of nights ago.'

However good Lindy Galton may have been

at body sculpture, she had no skills in the art of deception. 'How much do you know about it?' she blurted out.

'Well, clearly not as much as you do, Lindy. Which is why I'm asking you these questions.' Mrs Pargeter moved closer. '*Was* the girl on the third floor Jenny Hargreaves?'

Lindy Galton's mouth opened to reply, but she was distracted by a slight clang from above. They both looked over the top of the cubicle wall to the ladder from which Stan the Stapler was still doing his Dynorod routine.

The oddjob man was not looking at them, but he did seem almost too studiously pre-occupied with his task. The two women exchanged glances. 'Can't talk now,' Lindy Galton breathed. 'Later in the day.'

'All right. When?'

'Quarter past nine. Down here. Everyone else'll be involved in the Weigh-In.'

Mrs Pargeter gave a quick nod, as Lindy Galton crossed to cancel the 'Empty' switch and say in a voice that was suddenly loud, 'No, I'm very sorry, Mrs Pargeter, but I think it would be unwise. The salts and minerals in the mud could all too easily trigger off your allergy.'

With appropriate expressions of annoyance and frustration at this cruel deprivation, Mrs Pargeter left the Dead Sea Mud Bath unit.

Chapter Thirteen

There was another message to ring Mr Mason when she got back to her room. Truffler, as ever, had done his stuff. He'd tracked down Tom O'Brien, Jenny Hargreaves' boyfriend.

'How did you find him — through Cambridge?' asked Mrs Pargeter.

'No,' Truffler replied dolefully. 'I had to track him down by . . . other routes.'

She knew better than to enquire further. 'Any chance of my meeting him?'

'Oh yes, I've set it up. That is, if you'd be able to get out of that place for a while . . .'

'For heaven's sake, Truffler. Brotherton Hall isn't Colditz.' Though when she came to think of it, there were similarities.

'Good. Well, he said he could give us an hour at lunchtime today. In London, that'd be.'

'Great. Shall I book us into the Savoy Grill?'

'Erm. I don't think that'd be exactly young Mr O'Brien's style, Mrs Pargeter.'

Young Mr O'Brien's style proved to be a

90

greasy spoon café round the back of King's Cross Station. He and Truffler were tucking into the All-Day Breakfast — bacon, egg, sausage, tomatoes, beans, fried bread, and a huge mug of tea — when Mrs Pargeter arrived. Though she turned a few heads in her scarlet linen jacket over floral silk print, she did not look out of place. Mrs Pargeter had that rare quality in any surroundings of being always conspicuous, but never out of place.

After basic introductions, Truffler asked if he could order her anything. ' 'Fraid they probably won't have that much that'll fit in with your Brotherton Hall diet.'

'Oh well,' said Mrs Pargeter nobly, 'can't be helped.' She looked at their plates. 'I'll have the same as you.'

While Truffler vied with a couple of gas fitters for attention at the fat-smeared counter, Mrs Pargeter made a quick assessment of the boy opposite her.

He was good-looking, black hair slicked back, and pale blue eyes, which at that moment were giving her a sullen once-over. Tom O'Brien had not a spare ounce of fat on him. He wore a shapeless navy-blue raincoat over a black T-shirt and jeans, and sat in a defensive posture that firmly stated he was there under suffrance.

Mrs Pargeter smiled at him. 'I want to find

out about Jenny.'

'So do I,' he replied, the sourness in his tone accentuating a slight Irishness. 'That's why I'm here. Mr Mason said you had some information.'

This was difficult. The information Mrs Pargeter did have was the last information the boy would want to hear. Anyway, it was not information she could divulge. At that moment she couldn't be sure that the starved body she had seen was that of Jenny Hargreaves. She had only Ankle-Deep Arkwright's word to go on, and he was clearly lying about at least some aspects of the case.

Seeing the hunger for news in Tom O'Brien's face, for a moment Mrs Pargeter entertained the attractive idea that the body had not been Jenny's, that Ank had invented a name just to cloud the water.

But if that were the case, why had he come up with an address too? And an address which matched the name he had chosen?

This, Mrs Pargeter realized, was not the moment to pursue such questions. 'I don't so much have information,' she said gently, 'as maybe some pointers to where Jenny's been the last few months.'

Tom O'Brien was instantly alert. 'Well, that's more than I've managed to get. What have you found out?'

Truffler's return to the table, placing a large mug of tea in front of her, gave Mrs Pargeter a moment to shape her reply. 'It's just I've heard Jenny's name mentioned round Brotherton Hall . . . you know the place I mean?'

The contemptuous nod showed exactly what Tom O'Brien thought of health spas — and the kind of people who frequented them.

'I've heard rumours,' Mrs Pargeter went on, 'that Jenny may even have booked in there for a while.'

The interest faded from the boy's eyes. 'Well, they're crap rumours then. Even assuming Jenny would ever want to go to a place like that . . . And she wouldn't! Just because she's at Cambridge, don't imagine she's some bone-headed upper-class snob. Jenny's got her head firmly screwed on — she's not a class traitor like some of those social-climbing girls you meet at . . .' He realized he was getting off the subject. 'What I'm saying is there's no way she could have afforded to go to somewhere like Brotherton Hall. That was Jenny's problem, for God's sake — she didn't have any money.'

'But, just imagining for a moment that she somehow found the money . . .'

'If she'd found any money, there's a million other things she would have spent it on.'

'Or if someone had given her the stay at a health spa as a present . . .'

The thought he might have a rival brought a haunted look into Tom's eyes. 'Who?' he demanded. 'Do you know there was someone?'

'No, no, I'm just imagining. But what I really want to know is — would Jenny have had any reason to go to a health spa?'

The boy looked confused by the question.

'What Mrs Pargeter means,' Truffler elucidated, 'is — was Jenny fat?'

'Oh. No. Well, not particularly.' A distant hunger of recollection softened his words. 'She was . . . well-rounded and . . .' He cleared his throat. 'Certainly not thin, anyway.'

Mrs Pargeter tried to force from her mind the skeletal body she had seen on the trolley at Brotherton Hall. 'And she never expressed a desire to go to a health spa?'

'No, no, of course she didn't. She wouldn't have dared.'

'Why do you say that?'

'Because she knew I'd disapprove of poncy places like that.'

'And she wouldn't have done anything that you disapproved of?'

The question was casual, but Tom O'Brien

was instantly aware of its subtext. 'And I don't mean because I was a chauvinist, Mrs Pargeter. Jenny and I talked a lot, about everything. We thought alike about the really important things.'

'And what would you say *are* the really important things?'

There was no hesitation about his reply. The issues were ones he had thought through in great detail and about which he was passionate. 'The environment, obviously. That's the most important item on the world's agenda. If we don't get that sorted out, then it's all over for humankind. We've got to make people think differently. So long as their dominant motive remains profit and money-making, nothing's going to get any better. There'll be more poison pumped into the atmosphere, more forests cut down, more animal species sacrificed in the cause of consumerist experimentation. We've got to change the world whilst we still have a world left to change!'

Mrs Pargeter, though never an activist herself for any cause, could respect such fervour in others. And there was no doubting the boy's sincerity.

'So, in order to change the world, do you reckon you can use any methods?'

'Of course you can.'

'*Any* methods? I mean, even violence and terrorism?'

Tom O'Brien's lips set in a hard line. '*Particularly* violence and terrorism.'

'You think the end justifies the means?'

'It must do! If you stop and think of the violence that man's committed against the natural world, then a bit of necessary violence against man to restore the balance . . . well, it's a small price to pay.'

'And what kind of violence are you talking about? Sabotage? Bombings?'

'Yes.'

'Killing people?'

'Oh yes. When it's necessary,' Tom O'Brien replied with the quiet righteousness of the fanatic.

Chapter Fourteen

The boy's pale blue eyes suddenly darted sideways. Hope and yearning glowed in his face.

Mrs Pargeter followed his gaze through the café's steamed-up window to the street outside. Three girls passed by, tantalizingly slowly. Their strutting movements and the shortness of their skirts identified them as practitioners of the art for which King's Cross has become famous.

The hope had gone from Tom O'Brien's face as he looked back. Odd, was Mrs Pargeter's initial thought; why should a boy as good-looking as Tom waste his time gazing at prostitutes? Then light dawned.

'Going back to Jenny . . .' she began delicately. 'I want to know more about her.'

The interrogation was interrupted by the arrival of her steaming mound of All-Day Breakfast, swimming in enough fat to light the average Anglo-Saxon mead-hall for a decade. Mrs Pargeter looked at the plate with relish, sliced off a triangle of fried bread, which she loaded with tomato and beans and ate, before repeating, 'Yes, I want to know more about Jenny . . .'

Tom O'Brien looked truculent and suspicious. 'Why?'

'Because we're both trying to find her. If we pool our information, the chances of succeeding'll be that much better.'

He thought about this for a moment, before deciding in favour of co-operation. 'OK. What do you want to know?'

'You haven't seen her since the last week of last term?'

'No.'

'But you didn't have a row about anything just before she left?'

'Certainly not. We were very close.'

'No arguments at all?'

'No. Not what you'd call arguments.'

'What would you call them then?' asked Truffler bluntly. Mrs Pargeter took the opportunity of his interposition to load up and despatch another triangle of fried bread.

'Well . . .' Tom considered Truffler's question. 'Well, I suppose you'd call them disagreements. Disagreements about priorities.'

Mrs Pargeter continued her softer approach. 'What kind of priorities?'

'Money, mostly. How we should spend any money we'd got. Not that we had any, of course.'

'In what way did you disagree about that?'

'Well, I thought we should devote anything we had to the cause . . .'

'The environment?'

He nodded, but Mrs Pargeter had to prompt him to continue. 'And what did Jenny want to spend the money on?'

'She was . . . sort of . . .' He swallowed before the shamefaced confession. 'Deep down Jenny's a very conventional person, and I suppose, because she's grown up with her parents always being hard-up and that, she's a great believer in . . .' He could hardly bring himself to shape the alien word. *'Saving.'*

'Ah. What did she want to save for?'

'Oh . . .' He looked embarrassed. 'Sort of . . . you know . . . traditional things . . .'

'Like . . . getting married?' Mrs Pargeter suggested lightly.

His blush told her that she had scored a direct hit. 'Nothing wrong with that,' she said.

'Maybe not, but . . .' His words petered out. Mrs Pargeter could sympathize with his problem. To have a girlfriend of such mundane ambitions must have been a serious threat to the street credibility of a self-appointed anarchist like Tom O'Brien.

Time to move the enquiry on. Reluctantly deferring another mouthful of her All-Day Breakfast, Mrs Pargeter asked, 'And since that last week of term you haven't seen Jenny or heard from her?'

'Not directly, no.'

'What do you mean?'

'I did ring her parents once. Her old man managed to stay civil long enough to tell me she'd phoned them a couple of days before. But since then . . .'

'In fact,' said Truffler Mason, who could be surprisingly sensitive at times, 'I happen to know she's kept in touch with her parents right through. They last heard from her just before the university term started.'

Tom O'Brien seemed relieved by the news. Mrs Pargeter felt terrible about the other news that the young man might shortly have to hear.

'She didn't give any indication of where she was?' he asked eagerly.

'No. They got the impression she was doing some kind of holiday job, but they didn't know what or where.'

'That would be in character,' Tom mused.

'What do you mean?' asked Mrs Pargeter.

'Jenny's very proud. Neither of us had got any money, so it would have been in character for her to go off and get a job. No way would she ever ask for anything from anyone else — least of all from her parents. She knew how little they'd got. I'd hear her on the phone telling them how easily she was managing on

100

her grant — which was a load of crap. She didn't want them to be worried. I think she sometimes even sent them money that she certainly couldn't afford.'

'What's odd about the situation,' Mrs Pargeter ruminated, 'is not that Jenny should have got a job . . . but that she shouldn't have told you that she was getting one . . .' The boy nodded in downcast agreement. 'Can you think of any reasons why she might not have told you?'

His reply was drawn out of him reluctantly. 'Only the one.'

'And what's that?'

'That she didn't think I'd approve of the work she was doing.'

Mrs Pargeter understood immediately. She looked out of the window at a miniskirted girl brazenly chatting up a tourist in an anorak. 'That's why you're here, Tom, isn't it? You're afraid Jenny might have come down here to make money?'

'I couldn't think of anything else,' he mumbled. 'I had to look for her. I had to start somewhere.'

'So you've been round here, watching the girls come and go, for how long . . ?'

'I don't know . . . Two weeks . . . three weeks?' The confession had released some tension in him. He looked suddenly haggard with exhaustion.

'Where are you living?'

'Sleeping on someone's floor.'

'Whereabouts?'

She only got a shrug by way of answer.

'And that's why you haven't gone back to Cambridge?'

'I can't. I can't go back till I find Jenny.' He looked suddenly very young and vulnerable.

'But you mustn't ruin your life and your education for —'

Mrs Pargeter never got the chance to finish her sentence. Tom O'Brien's attention had been caught by another group of miniskirted girls hurrying past the café window. 'I must go!' he blurted. Then, showing his good upbringing, he added from the door, 'Are you sure you don't mind paying for the lunch?'

Truffler gestured acquiescence and the boy was gone. 'Shall I go after him, Mrs Pargeter?'

She shook her head and speared a sausage. 'No point. I think we've got all we can from him. And, anyway, Truffler, if you've found him once, I'm sure you can . . .'

The detective's nod of confidence made the rest of her sentence redundant.

Mrs Pargeter finished her mouthful of sausage in reflective mood. 'Poor kid. He's clearly deeply in love with her.'

'Hm . . .'

'Or *was* deeply in love with her. You know what we've got to do next, don't you, Truffler?'

He probably did, but was polite enough to respect the rhetorical nature of her question.

'We've got to make certain that the dead girl I saw really was Jenny Hargreaves.'

Truffler Mason nodded, his conjecture proved correct.

'What about the parents?' asked Mrs Pargeter suddenly. 'Surely the hospital must have been in touch with them by now?'

'No, that's the odd thing,' said Truffler. 'I was going to tell you. Mr and Mrs Hargreaves still haven't heard anything.'

'Oh dear. Truffler, get in touch with all the hospitals in the Brotherton Hall area! As quickly as possible!'

Mrs Pargeter had suddenly turned very pale. And after Truffler had rushed off to follow her instructions, she didn't even feel up to finishing her All-Day Breakfast.

Which may be taken as a measure of how upset she was.

Chapter Fifteen

'Gary . . .' said Mrs Pargeter thoughtfully, as the limousine sped through the outer suburbs, 'if you discovered that your wife was doing a job —'

'Which I never would,' the uniformed chauffeur interrupted. 'Old-fashioned it may be, but I believe a bloke should bring home enough for his missus and the nippers without her having to go out to work.'

Others might have been surprised to hear these reactionary sentiments from such a young man, but Mrs Pargeter had long been aware of Gary's Victorian values.

'No, but if you did . . .' she persisted, 'what kind of work would your wife most want to keep secret from you?'

'What, like what kind of work would she least want me to find out about?' queried Gary, who liked to be in possession of all the facts before committing himself to an opinion on anything.

'That's it, yes.'

'Anything illegal,' the chauffeur pronounced, without a moment's hesitation.

Ah, the late Mr Pargeter had taught his protégé well. It could have been her husband himself speaking, Mrs Pargeter reflected fondly, thinking back to the punctilious care with which he had kept her innocent almost of the fact that crime existed in this wicked world. 'What you don't know about, my dear,' had been one of his regular sayings, 'you're in no position to tell anyone else about.'

Gary had clearly absorbed the same values. Mrs Pargeter could not help once again contemplating the wide influence her husband had exercised. All over the world were men and women, many of whom had taken a change of career direction in mid-life, who owed all their success to the training bestowed by the late Mr Pargeter.

Gary was a good example. Her husband had discovered the boy at the age of sixteen in a young offenders' centre, where he had been committed for joy-riding. The late Mr Pargeter had taken the boy under his wing, gently showed him the pointlessness of random car-theft, and paid for him to have driving lessons. The boy had felt ready after one, but his mentor insisted on two full courses of lessons before Gary was allowed to take his test.

The result, Mrs Pargeter mused as the limousine slid through the Surrey countryside, was the safest driver she had ever encountered.

The late Mr Pargeter, philanthropic as ever, had also put the boy through Advanced Motorist's instruction, and paid for him to take courses in speed and skid-control (even going to the lengths of having him trained to cope with the additional weight-hazard of an armoured car).

Then, when Gary was proficient, the late Mr Pargeter had been good enough to find work for him in his organization, work which tested the boy's skill to the full. His boss's confidence was never once shown to be misplaced. Gary's speed and repertoire of evasive manoeuvres had frequently saved other of the late Mr Pargeter's associates from the kind of accident that could have put them out of circulation for two or three years (or in some cases up to fifteen).

When his boss died, Gary, after an appropriate period of mourning, had set up a driving business of his own with a more public profile than had been accorded to his previous work. Mrs Pargeter, always a great supporter of new business enterprise, had backed the venture from the start, booking Gary on every occasion that she might possibly need a driver.

He had at first tried to refuse payment for his services, saying, 'After all, when I think how much I owe your late husband, it's the least I can do for his widow to —'

But Mrs Pargeter had interrupted him firmly, insisting she always would pay for everything. 'Neither a lender nor a borrower be,' she had said, quoting another of the late Mr Pargeter's regular sayings (though he may perhaps have borrowed that one from someone else).

So it was that she had organized Gary to drive her from Brotherton Hall to King's Cross, and to have the limousine on hand to return her after the meeting with Tom O'Brien.

Gary, who was used to ferrying Mrs Pargeter to more elegant venues than the greasy spoon, had been far too discreet to pass any comment.

'No, but give me a bit more detail,' Mrs Pargeter insisted. 'What kind of job would your wife least like you to know she was doing?'

'Not absolutely clear what you mean, Mrs Pargeter.'

'Well, for instance, would the worst thing you could find out be that . . . that she was on the game, for example?'

'I wouldn't like that much,' Gary conceded judiciously, 'but that wouldn't be the worst.'

'What would then?'

'The worst,' he said, 'the absolute worst —

the thing that'd really make me divorce her on the spot and never see her again — would be if . . .'

'Yes?'

'If I found she'd gone and joined the police.'

'Ah. Yes. Well, of course.'

Somehow Mrs Pargeter didn't think she was going to get much stimulus to her thinking about Jenny Hargreaves's job from Gary.

On her return to Brotherton Hall, she bumped into an ecstatic Kim Thurrock — or it might be more accurate to say an ecstatic Kim Thurrock bumped into her. Kim was rushing from the gym, where she'd spent an hour increasing her weight-training circuits and repetitions, to the swimming-pool, where she still had thirty lengths to complete.

The cause of her ecstasy was quickly revealed. 'I didn't see you this morning. Do you know, Melita, at the Seven-Thirty Weigh-In, I'd lost another ounce and a half!'

Mrs Pargeter uttered suitable expressions of amazement.

'I mean, I really do *feel* thinner. Don't you reckon I *look* thinner!'

Kim stood sideways, holding her tummy in, for her friend's appraisal.

Mrs Pargeter found it difficult to come up with an opinion. She'd never given much thought to Kim Thurrock's figure — it had always seemed perfectly all right to her — so she had difficulty judging to what extent (if any) it had changed.

And Kim's now-permanent uniform of *Mind Over Fatty Matter* leotard and leggings (oh yes, and presumably exercise bra) didn't make assessment any easier. The patterns on the garments looked wonderful on Sue Fisher herself, and on her team of aerobic robots, but then presumably they had the kind of bodies that would look good in bin-liners. On ordinary bodies, like Kim Thurrock's, however, the pattern seemed to have a different effect; almost as if it had been expressly designed to accentuate any minor bulges.

As she learned more about the *Mind Over Fatty Matter* approach to marketing, Mrs Pargeter found this conjecture increasingly plausible. It would be in character for Sue Fisher to promote garments which actually made people look fatter. They would preserve that all-important distance between the ideal and the reality, encourage her punters' basic dislike of their own bodies, and ensure that they bought even more *Mind Over Fatty Matter* products to make up for their shortcomings.

'You look very nice, Kim love,' said Mrs Pargeter comfortingly.

'*Nice?*' Kim Thurrock echoed. 'But do I look *thin?*'

What did the truth matter under such circumstances? 'Very thin, love,' Mrs Pargeter reassured her.

'Oh, good.' But Kim still looked uncertain.

'Really terrific. I bet you're learning to love that body of yours now, aren't you, love?'

'Good heavens, *no!* I'm still *such* a mess. There's still *so* much to do.'

So the *Mind Over Fatty Matter* programme of stimulating feelings of inadequacy was still doing its stuff.

'But do you know the other wonderful thing that happened today?' Kim asked.

'No,' said Mrs Pargeter, who didn't.

'I bought a prepublication copy of the *Mind Over Fatty Matter Book of Warm Salads . . .*'

'Well, well . . .'

'And do you know what?'

'No,' said Mrs Pargeter, who didn't.

'Sue Fisher actually signed it for me!'

'I didn't know she was still here.'

'Well, she certainly was this morning. And she's so generous. She signed books for practically everyone.'

After they'd paid for them, Mrs Pargeter thought cynically. Curious, she asked, 'What did she write in yours?'

' "Keep trying, Kim!" ' her friend replied proudly.

Clever. Never write 'Well done'. Never imply the process is complete. Because, of course, a slimmer who's achieved her goal is going to stop buying *Mind Over Fatty Matter* products, isn't she?

'Anyway, I must dash. I've still got these thirty lengths to do.' Kim stopped, suddenly solicitous. 'And how's your programme going, Melita?'

'Programme?'

'Yes. Fitness, slimming, you know . . .'

'Ah. Well, I'm doing as much as the allergy allows me to,' she replied in a bravely martyred tone.

'Oh, you do have rotten luck,' Kim sympathized.

'I know, but . . . well . . .'

'*C'est la vie,*' Kim supplied, drawing once again on her evening classes.

'Exactly. Still, I live in hope,' Mrs Pargeter continued with spirit. 'Only ate half my portion at lunchtime today.'

'Oh. Well *done,*' said Kim Thurrock.

Chapter Sixteen

Mrs Pargeter ate her full portion of dinner in the 'Allergy Room' that evening. Though still anxious about the news she was expecting from Truffler Mason, she could see no point in spoiling two meals in a row.

Anyway, she owed it to Gaston to do justice to his *Entrecôte à la Bordelaise* and *Crêpe à la Mode d'Orléans*. It seemed a pity to let any of the Crozes Hermitage go to waste either. And since Gaston had cooked some *petit fours* specially to go with her coffee, it would have been churlish not to try them.

In spite of her forebodings, she was in a state of excitement. At last her investigation seemed to be getting somewhere. Truffler would soon be able to tell her whether the body she had seen *was* that of Jenny Hargreaves.

And then of course she was due to find out more from Lindy Galton in the Dead Sea Mud Bath unit at nine-fifteen.

She lingered over her last *petit four*, checking her watch in a desultory way and waiting till she heard the nervous giggling of guests scuttling to the gym to experience their day's final humiliation at the Nine O'Clock Weigh-In.

The sounds subsided, and Brotherton Hall was filled with a silence thick as fog, while Mrs Pargeter made her way to the Dead Sea Mud Bath unit.

Down there, too, all was nearly silent. Only the soft swish of the rotor blade in its tank of mud provided a rhythm that gave texture to the silence.

The lights were on, but there was no sign of anyone in the central area surrounded by the four cubicles.

All the doors were shut. Mrs Pargeter opened one and looked in. The cubicle contained nothing but its spotlessly gleaming bath.

The contents of the second were identical.

The third cubicle, however, was full of Dead Sea Mud.

It wasn't just the bath that was full. The outline of that had been lost in the brown sludge which lay thickly over the floor and oozed through the opened doorway to Mrs Pargeter's neatly shod feet.

She moved back from the encroaching tide and looked towards the control console on the wall. The 'Fill' switch was in its 'Off' position.

From the sluice at the bath's head a single stalactite of mud depended.

Mrs Pargeter was about to turn away to check the last cubicle when she realized that there was something half-submerged in the mud.

It took a moment to work out what it was. A small archipelago of rounded, mud-slimed promontaries broke the surface. And there, against what was presumably the side of the bath, protruded something like a bedraggled marsh plant.

A catch of horror clasped at her throat as she took in what it really was.

A muddy hand!

Mrs Pargeter removed her shoes and stepped forward as quickly as she dared over the treacherous surface. She felt voracious mud close over her feet, instantly penetrating her tights and squeezing obscenely between her toes. Clutching a rail and testing each foot-step to keep her from plunging into the bath itself, she edged forward.

Bracing herself with one arm against the rail she reached for the body and tried to pull it upwards. But she could get no purchase on the slimy limbs, which kept slopping back into the mud.

At last she contrived a grip under the neck and raised the head above the surface. Mud slipped glutinously back off the features and clogged hair.

But not enough mud slipped off to make an identification.

Mrs Pargeter had to wipe at the filthy slime with a towel before she could recognize the face.

Lindy Galton.

The girl's mouth gaped open. Inside, it was full of the Dead Sea Mud that had asphyxiated her.

Chapter Seventeen

There was a house phone in the central area with a sheet of internal numbers stuck on the wall beside it. Mrs Pargeter rang Ankle-Deep Arkwright's extension, but there was no reply.

She got through to Reception and announced, with considerable self-restraint, that there had been 'an accident' in the Dead Sea Mud Bath unit. The receptionist, using those perky upward inflections with which girls at reception school are trained to greet pools wins and pogroms alike, assured her that 'someone will be down as soon as possible, madam'.

Mrs Pargeter had no thought of leaving the unit. There was mud all over her, but cleaning-up would have to wait. A series of mountingly unpleasant conjectures about the causes of Lindy Galton's death built up in her head.

She had made one more attempt to get the corpse out of the bath, to give it a little dignity in death, but then given up. Probably better to leave things as they were, anyway, for the inevitable police enquiry.

116

So, while increasingly disturbing thoughts erupted in her mind, Mrs Pargeter sat on a bench and waited to see who would be 'down as soon as possible'.

It was Dr Potter.

He was as dapper as ever. A double-breasted suit in Prince of Wales check over his angular frame, suede shoes whose distinctive shape proclaimed them to be hand-made.

He took in Mrs Pargeter's presence before he looked at Cubicle Three, from which mud was still inexorably advancing over the immaculate tiles.

'What seems to be the trouble?' he asked. (Presumably doctors are so conditioned to using that question that they have difficulty in framing others.) 'Reception said there had been some kind of accident.'

'Yes.' Mrs Pargeter pointed to the open cubicle door and the mud-spattered area beyond.

Dr Potter looked across and his thin face pursed with annoyance. 'If there's something wrong with the sluices, that would appear to be a job for a plumber rather than a doctor.'

'It's not just the sluices. There's a body in the mud.'

'What?' He turned his silt-coloured eyes on her in amazement.

'Lindy Galton. She's under that lot — drowned.'

Dr Potter tutted, like a bureaucrat who's found a form incorrectly filled in. 'Oh really! This kind of thing happens far too often at Brotherton Hall, you know.'

'What — people getting killed?' Mrs Pargeter asked eagerly, thinking she really was on to something this time.

Dr Potter quickly disabused her. 'No. Staff using the facilities without permission. It happens in the gym, in the swimming-pool, everywhere. And the trouble is, they do it at times when the facilities aren't properly supervized, which raises terrible problems with insurance. It's been inevitable that something like this would happen one day.' He tutted again, then added as an afterthought, 'You're sure she *is* dead?'

'Well, she looked dead to me, but then I'm not an expert.'

'No.'

Mrs Pargeter waited in vain for him to pick up the prompt, so continued, 'Whereas you are. I'd have thought the first thing a doctor should have done would be to pull the body out and try to revive her.'

'Don't you start telling me what I should have done, Mrs Pargeter!' But her words had had some effect. 'Yes, I suppose I'd better take a look at her,' he conceded reluctantly. After a moment's hesitation, he removed his jacket, folded it neatly on to a bench and started towards the cubicle.

'Surely you're going to take your shoes off?' said Mrs Pargeter. 'That stuff'll ruin them.'

'Whether I choose to ruin my shoes or not is, I would have thought, my decision, Mrs Pargeter,' he said, placing a suede-clad foot firmly into the mud, which rose to cover it.

'Yes, yes, of course.'

Oblivious to the splashes on his clothes, Dr Potter took hold of the rail and reached down to grab the body. With surprising strength, he dragged Lindy Galton out of the bath in one movement, then slid her along to the central area. The manhandling scraped enough mud off to show that the girl had been naked when she got into the bath.

Dr Potter bent over the body. No pulse-listening or breath-checking. Not even the thought of resuscitation.

Just a quick look, and he turned to the wall telephone.

He got an outside line and barked instructions about collecting the body to whoever answered him.

'Was that the police?' Mrs Pargeter asked as he put the receiver down.

'The hospital.'

'Shouldn't we call the police?'

'After an accident like this it is usual to call the hospital first. They may be able to do something.'

'Something you couldn't do?'

'I don't understand you, Mrs Pargeter.' The dull eyes flickered a cold look at her.

'Well, look, you're a doctor. Either she's dead . . . or there's something that can be done for her. If there's something that can be done, it would stand more chance of succeeding if you did it here — now.'

He moved closer to her and lowered his voice. 'I don't think you quite realize what is at stake here, Mrs Pargeter. Brotherton Hall is a substantial business, and one whose reputation could be seriously affected by something like this. I can assure you we are not going to let an accident caused by one of the staff abusing her position here jeopardize the company's future.'

'So you think it'd be simpler to have Lindy Galton registered "Dead on Arrival" at the hospital, rather than having the police in here inspecting the scene where she actually died?'

'Exactly, Mrs Pargeter. You show a very acute understanding of the situation.'

'And is that what happened with Jenny Hargreaves?' she asked coolly.

'I don't know who you're talking about.'

The response was immediate. The name prompted no flicker of recognition.

'She was a girl —'

'All I do know,' Dr Potter steamrollered over her, 'is that a lot of people have a lot of investment riding on Brotherton Hall; and that anyone who threatened the success of this enterprise would . . . would be very unwise.'

This limp second thought about how to finish the sentence was more chilling than if he had actually spelt out the threat.

Chapter Eighteen

Mrs Pargeter was lost in thought as she walked slowly up to her room. So lost that she didn't see Kim Thurrock until her friend was right alongside her in the ill-lit corridor. (The corridors at Brotherton Hall were all lit in a manner which the interior designer had described as 'discreetly modern', but which came across as old-fashioned murky.)

'Three ounces less tonight!' Kim announced in triumph.

'Oh, great. Well done,' Mrs Pargeter responded absently.

'Three ounces! Even the girl who was monitoring my weighing said congratulations.'

Oh dear, she'll be out on her ear tomorrow, thought Mrs Pargeter. Commendation of a guest's progress at Brotherton Hall was as heinous a staff crime as a scowl in Disneyland.

'And, what's more, I actually got the address of this plastic surgeon in Harley Street.'

'Oh, for Heaven's sake, love. You're not still thinking of that, are you?'

'It's worth just investigating the possibilities,' Kim pleaded. 'I mean, the first consultation with this Mr Littlejohn is totally free.'

'But any other dealings with him are no doubt totally expensive.'

'Well . . .' Kim Thurrock was still childlike in her enthusiasm. 'It can't do any harm just to find out a bit more . . .'

'So long as you promise me you won't start anything before Thicko comes out — I mean, is back with you.'

'There's no danger of that. He'll be home in a couple of weeks. But it would be nice,' Kim added wistfully, 'if I'd had my first consultation by then . . .'

'So that Thicko can see what's on offer? You show him Mr Littlejohn's brochure of available bums and get him to choose the one he'd like to see on you — is that it?'

'No, of course not,' said Kim, in a way that meant exactly the opposite.

'Well, look, don't you rush into anything, love. Give Thicko time to readjust to you as you are before you go changing yourself — eh?'

'Yes, of course, Melita.' Kim gave a little giggle of excitement. 'Ooh, I can't believe he'll be back home so soon.'

'He will be. And you'll have a wonderful time,' said Mrs Pargeter, fondly remembering many comparable reunions with the late Mr Pargeter.

Her mood was more sombre as she sat in her bedroom and thought about Lindy Galton's murder.

Because there was no other word she would use to describe it. Dr Potter's ready acceptance of the 'accident' explanation had been dictated by concern for the Brotherton Hall business empire — or possibly even darker motives.

But it had not been an accident. Lindy Galton was far too familiar with the workings of the Dead Sea Mud Baths to make a mistake of over-filling one.

Anyway, in spite of what Dr Potter had said about the girl taking advantage of the facilities for her own benefit, Mrs Pargeter knew that Lindy Galton would never voluntarily have gone into the bath, because of her allergic reaction to the mud it contained.

Which meant that someone must have pushed her in. Or, more probably, hit her over the head first and then pushed her in.

What sickened Mrs Pargeter about the murder was the thought that she could have been responsible for it. Obviously not responsible for killing Lindy Galton, but for the fact that she had been killed.

Mrs Pargeter had asked for information about Jenny Hargreaves and Lindy had fixed to meet her by the Dead Sea Mud Baths that evening. It was horribly possible that the girl had been murdered to prevent that meeting from taking place.

Their fixing of the tryst could easily have been overheard. Mrs Pargeter concentrated, trying to visualize the morning's scene.

Stan the Stapler had certainly been present, on his ladder, clearing the obstruction in the mud tank.

And there had been three other people, one in the bath, one drying under the sunlamp, and the third scrubbing off in the shower. They were all potential witnesses, but in each case, so complete had been their covering of mud, Mrs Pargeter could not even specify the suspect's gender.

The telephone's ringing broke in on her gloomy thoughts.

'Hello?'

'Mrs Pargeter, it's Truffler.'

'Have you checked the hospitals?'

He dismally confirmed that he had.

'*And?*'

'And — nothing, I'm afraid.'

'What — you mean Jenny Hargreaves' body wasn't taken to any of them?'

'No. And, if I may anticipate your next

question, no body of a young girl who had died of anorexia has been taken to any of them for the past two years.'

'Oh,' said Mrs Pargeter, as new thoughts started to swirl in her head. 'Oh.'

'Is there anything else I can do?' he asked. 'Any further investigation?'

'Yes,' she replied slowly. 'Could you get back on to the hospitals — tomorrow morning it'd better be — and find out if any of them has taken delivery of another girl's body?'

'Another anorexia victim?'

'No. This one died of asphyxiation. And her name was Lindy Galton.'

'Right you are. I'll let you know as soon as I've got anything.'

Mrs Pargeter sat in her room for a long time that night, lost in thought. But it wasn't the kind of thought she enjoyed being lost in.

Chapter Nineteen

Truffler got back to her early the following morning, the Thursday. Lindy Galton — or rather the mortal and muddy remains of Lindy Galton — had been taken to one of the local hospitals the night before, and there — surprise, surprise — she had been certified 'Dead on Arrival'.

As yet, Truffler had not been able to find out what level of investigation would be conducted into the 'accident' at Brotherton Hall, though Mrs Pargeter was not anticipating anything very rigorous. She felt certain there would be a cover-up — which, considering the circumstances of Lindy Galton's demise, was perhaps an unfortunate expression.

So the two deaths had been treated differently. Though Mrs Pargeter had no doubt that both were suspicious, Lindy Galton's had gone through the official channels, while the body of Jenny Hargreaves had apparently disappeared off the face of the earth.

Assuming that it *was* the body of Jenny Hargreaves. Particularly since she had met Tom O'Brien, Mrs Pargeter couldn't repress her hope that the girl who had starved to death had been someone else. She only had Ankle-Deep Arkwright's assurance on the identity of the corpse, and he had certainly not been telling the complete truth.

She knew from her own checking of the computer that 'Jenny Hargreaves' ' registration document had been invalid and, although death had removed the opportunity of confirming her suspicions, Mrs Pargeter felt convinced that Lindy Galton had falsified the record on Ankle-Deep Arkwright's orders.

But, if Ank's aim was simply to obscure the identity of the first dead girl, why had he used the name and address of a real person? The fabrication of a name would have left no leads to be followed.

It was becoming increasingly urgent for Mrs Pargeter to have a straight talk to Ankle-Deep Arkwright.

He wasn't in his office. The girl on Reception said that Mr Arkwright would be away for a few days. No, she was afraid she couldn't say where. But his absence would have no effect on Mrs Pargeter's status at Brotherton Hall. Mr Arkwright had been very insistent before he left that Mrs Pargeter's 'Special Treatment' should continue and that all the facilities of the 'Allergy Room' should be at her disposal for the remaining days of her stay.

It reeked to Mrs Pargeter of guilty conscience. Ankle-Deep Arkwright's message was effectively saying, 'I'm going to be away until after you've left Brotherton Hall, so you won't be able to ask me any awkward questions; but, to show there are no hard feelings between us, I'm making it possible for you to enjoy the rest of your time here.'

Just as she was about to leave Reception, Mrs Pargeter had another thought and asked the girl where she might find Stan the oddjob man (she didn't know how official his nickname 'Stan the Stapler' was). But there again she drew a blank. 'Mr Bristow' had a few days' leave owing to him and would not be back until after the weekend.

Maybe it was all coincidence, but Mrs Pargeter couldn't help sensing a conspiracy to block her investigation. Lindy Galton was dead and the other people she wanted to talk to were suddenly unavailable. She supposed she could try to get more information out of Dr Potter, but wasn't optimistic of success. He had been less than forthcoming in the Dead Sea Mud Bath unit the previous evening.

What distressed her most about the situation was the involvement of Ank. How deeply he was in she didn't know, but she reckoned this time it was well above the ankles.

And that hurt. She had had dealings with a great many of the late Mr Pargeter's associates since his death, and had found in every one of them unswerving loyalty and willingness to provide any services she might require. The thought of Ankle-Deep Arkwright being deliberately obstructive to her was an unattractive one.

Still, she concluded with weary philosophy, it wouldn't be the first time. The late Mr Pargeter had given his complete trust to Julian Embridge — and look what happened in Streatham.

'Well, Ank always had an eye for the main chance,' Truffler conceded cautiously. 'Was prepared to do some nifty footwork to get out of one set-up into another that looked more profitable, if you know what I mean.'

'Yes, I do.' Mrs Pargeter's hand played restlessly with the cord of the telephone. 'It's just the change in his behaviour was so sudden. He was all over me until I told him about having seen the body, then he clammed up. Which must mean he had something to do with the girl's death, mustn't it?'

'Not necessarily. Could just mean that he knew a corpse was bad for business and wanted it hushed up.'

'Yes. Oh, it's so frustrating.' Mrs Pargeter looked out of her window to the front drive of Brotherton Hall, where she had seen the ambulance only a few nights before. 'If only I could talk to someone else who saw Jenny Hargreaves' body . . . I even have moments when I start wondering if I imagined it.'

'Mrs Pargeter . . .' Reproach made Truffler's voice sound even more funereal. 'This doesn't sound like the Mrs Pargeter I know and love. I've never before heard you not being sure about things.'

'No, you're absolutely right. Not my normal style at all. I must snap out of it.' She did, and her tone changed instantly. 'Truffler, I want you to find out where Ank's gone. Can you do that?'

'Mrs Pargeter —'

She stopped the tone of reproach from intensifying. 'Sorry, shouldn't have asked. Right, if you could find out where Ank is now, and if he's been anywhere else in the last twenty-four hours . . ? And could you do the same for Stan the Stapler? I need to talk to him too.'

'No problem, Mrs Pargeter. Anything else?'

'Erm . . . Dr Potter. Yes, I'd be glad of any background you can get on Dr Potter.'

'Leave it with me.'

'And I suppose the other question we ought to be asking is — if Jenny Hargreaves' body wasn't taken to a hospital . . .'

'Hm?'

'Where was it taken?'

Mrs Pargeter's uncharacteristic lapse of confidence was quickly behind her. Suddenly she felt more positive. And she realized that there was one very simple piece of investigation she could do straight away.

The girl at Reception made no demur about giving her the Dead Sea Mud Bath booking sheets.

'Just want to see if I can fit another one in before I go. Felt so terrific after the last one I had,' Mrs Pargeter lied breezily. 'There aren't any problems with the baths at the moment, are there?'

The girl looked blank. 'No. Why should there be?'

'I thought I heard one of the staff saying there'd been a mess-up last night with a bath getting clogged up or something . . ?'

'First I've heard of it.' So the news of Lindy Galton's death had, so far at least, been kept from the rest of the Brotherton Hall staff. 'No, they would have told me if there'd been any problem.'

The telephone's ringing conveniently diverted the receptionist's attention. Mrs Pargeter stopped looking at the current booking sheet and flipped back to the day before. She wanted to identify the three mud-camouflaged guests who, along with Stan the Stapler, might have overheard her arranging to meet Lindy Galton.

Her own bath had been booked for ten o'clock. Other guests were booked in, two at nine and one at nine-thirty.

The first two names, presumably belonging to the person who had been drying off under the sunlamp and the one in the shower, were unfamiliar.

But the third, the name of the mud-covered figure in Cubicle One, did mean something to Mrs Pargeter.

It was 'Sue Fisher'.

Chapter Twenty

That day was the first time that Mrs Pargeter had entertained in the 'Allergy Room', but Gaston had been delighted when she mooted the idea. The prospect of having a larger audience for his underused gastronomic skills made him really push the boat out.

They started with *Pâté de Lièvre aux Pruneaux*, followed by an unfussy but perfect *Lobster Thermidor*, and rounded the meal off with *Millefeuille de Poire*. Two bottles of Pouilly-Fuissé eased along the main courses, and a rather fine Beaume de Venise animated the dessert.

Mrs Pargeter's guest, professionally blasé from lavish daily entertaining by public relations companies desperate for her attentions, was impressed.

Ellie Fenchurch had changed considerably from the time that the late Mr Pargeter had plucked her from a journalism course at a provincial polytechnic. Then she had been a gangly teenager, all sharp angles and awkward questions. Now her sharp angles were accentuated by breathtakingly expensive designer clothes, and for asking awkward questions she was paid a six-figure salary by one of the national Sunday newspapers.

Her weekly full-page interview was a monument to bitchiness. Her victims were flayed and exposed in all their rawness to the reading public. Their achievements were diminished, their private lives vilified, their mannerisms ridiculed, and their most deeply held beliefs presented as affectations. No one had come through unscathed from the blowtorch of Ellie Fenchurch's interview technique.

And an unending stream of international celebrities queued up to experience the humiliation.

'No problem,' she had said when Mrs Pargeter had rung up and suggested meeting. 'I'm meant to be interviewing Warren Beatty over lunch, but I'm sure he'll be over here again in the next decade or so — don't you worry about it.'

'Oh, but surely — ?' Mrs Pargeter had remonstrated. 'I mean, it doesn't have to be today it —'

'Of course it has to be today,' Ellie snapped back. 'When I think of how much your late husband did for me . . .'

'Well, if you're sure . . . I'll see at least you get a decent lunch out of it.'

'Mrs Pargeter, I'd help you for a Quarter-pounder and Small Fries,' said the woman who made it a point of honour always to send the wine back at the Connaught.

Ellie Fenchurch knew Brotherton Hall well. She'd never availed herself of the health spa's services, but she could quote precisely which treatments various major celebrities had undergone there — along with their weight loss or gain to the last fraction of an ounce.

In the same way she could enumerate the cosmetic operations of the famous — who'd had a hair transplant, who'd had a nose-job, who'd had liposuction, who'd had silicone implants, even (and this name surprised Mrs Pargeter) who'd had a penis-augmentation implant.

Ellie's list of celebrity addictions, adulteries, and sexual perversions was equally comprehensive.

It was for gleeful revelations such as these that every Sunday thousands of readers tossed aside the agglomeration of sections and supplements which surrounded it to home in first on her column.

But no one would have believed that the steel-clawed termagant of the Sundays was the same woman who sat, docile in the 'Allergy Room' of Brotherton Hall, floating in a haze

136

of Beaume-de-Venise-tinted nostalgia.

'Oh, when I think how much he did for me . . . He really taught me everything I know about the press. And he was so gentle, such a wonderful teacher. No, if anyone ever asked for the definition of a good man, they'd have to look no further than your husband.'

Mrs Pargeter indulged in a moment of moist-eyed agreement.

'And he was such an innovator,' Ellie enthused on. 'I think he was probably the first person fully to realize the importance of public relations in his particular line of business. And he did it with such subtlety. I mean there have been imitators — of course, every mould-breaking pioneer's going to have imitators — but none of them had the finesse of your husband. The manipulation of the press by someone like . . . say, Robert Maxwell, just looks crude by comparison. No, the late Mr Pargeter was the guv'nor.'

His widow, still moist-eyed, nodded.

'And I was just so lucky to be the beneficiary of all that wisdom. He took me from nothing and he gave me everything. He showed me how to get the stories that mattered, the kind of exposure that counted. I mean, the things he managed to get in the gossip columns . . . some of the stuff was just breath-taking.'

Another sentimental nod from Mrs Pargeter.

'I think his triumph was the Princess of Wales. Oh, a real coup that was. I mean, to get William Hickey to print a story about a certain young man being seen dancing at Annabel's with "herself" — at the very time when the young man in question was . . . what shall we say . . . *very differently occupied* in Milton Keynes . . . Oh, and knowing that the Palace is never going to issue a denial or anything like that. That was just the best, the most public alibi I've ever come across. Brilliant.'

'But you were the one who actually fed the story to William Hickey, weren't you?' said Mrs Pargeter, modestly spreading her late husband's glory.

'Yes. But the concept was his. Magic. Wonderful. No, by my definition, that was sheer genius.'

'Well, thank you very much.'

There was a silence, a moment of respect for the late Mr Pargeter's departed genius.

Ellie Fenchurch broke it. 'Anyway, Mrs Pargeter, what can I do for you? You name it — anything. You have only to say and it's done.'

'Well . . .' Mrs Pargeter took another sip of the Beaume de Venise as she gathered her

138

thoughts. 'There is a celebrity whom I need to have investigated . . .'

Ellie's eyes sparkled. 'Great. You've got the right person for any of that kind of stuff.'

'Yes. That's what I thought. The fact is, I need to find out some fairly private things about this celebrity . . .'

'Keep talking. This is meat and drink to me.'

'Things this celebrity will probably be unwilling to divulge . . .'

'You're talking to the person who made a certain Cabinet Minister admit to his nappy-wearing habit, Mrs Pargeter.'

'Yes. Yes, of course I am. Well, I just wondered . . . whether you'd be willing to help me in my investigation . . ?'

'The answer's been yes from the moment I first met your husband. Who is it I'm after?' the journalist asked eagerly.

'Sue Fisher.'

'Oh yes. Yes . . .'

And a new light came into Ellie Fenchurch's eye. It was the light that comes into a fox's eye in the moment between grabbing a chicken's neck and breaking it.

Chapter Twenty-One

'Stan Bristow . . .' said Mrs Pargeter as the limousine sped towards the south coast on the Friday morning.

'Who?' asked Gary.

'Stan the Stapler.'

'Oh, him — right.'

'Did you come across him much when he was working with my husband?'

'Sure. He was always around in the early days. Mr Fixit he was — done the lot. Not the brightest — couldn't talk, you probably know that — but a useful type to have on your side.'

'Yes. There's something odd about him, though . . .'

'How's that then? You come across him again, have you, Mrs Pargeter?'

'He's working at Brotherton Hall.'

'Oh. Good old Ank. There's loyalty. Keeping it in the family, eh?'

'Hm.'

'What do you mean about him being odd, though, Mrs Pargeter?'

'Well, I've come across a good few of my

late husband's associates over the years — some I've specifically contacted, some I've just met by chance — and they've all had one thing in common. As soon as they've discovered who I am, they all say how delighted they are to see me and how much they owe to my husband's kindness to them.'

'That's no surprise, Mrs Pargeter. I mean he was a prince among men, your husband, no question about it.'

'No . . .' She resolutely pushed nostalgia from her mind. 'Stan the Stapler's the exception, though. He must know who I am — can't *not* know who I am, but he hasn't given any sign of recognizing me. I know he can't talk, but . . . Well, I'd swear that he's deliberately avoided me. Can you think of any reason why he might have done that?'

'Well . . .' The chauffeur straightened his peaked cap. 'Maybe he's just shy or . . .'

'There's more to it, isn't there?' There was an uncomfortable silence followed by throat clearing from the front seat. 'You said Stan was always around "in the early days", Gary . . .'

'Yes.'

'Meaning that he wasn't around so much towards the end?'

'No. No, Thicko Thurrock took over a lot of his duties after . . .'

Gary wasn't finding this easy. Again his words trickled away.

'After what?'

'Well . . .'

'After Streatham, was it?' asked Mrs Pargeter with a flash of intuition.

Awkwardly the chauffeur admitted that she was right. After Streatham Stan the Stapler had not been so much in evidence in the late Mr Pargeter's business empire.

'But did anyone ever point a finger at him? Did anyone have any proof that he'd been involved in . . . in what went wrong?'

'No, no. No proof. Just a few suspicions was round at the time. Not that your husband'd have any of it. After he come out — I mean, when he was back in circulation — your husband wouldn't have anyone say a word against Stan, said he still stood by all his staff, would be happy to work with Stan again any time. You know, Mrs Pargeter . . .' He paused, assembling his words with the maximum delicacy. 'If there was any criticism I might ever make of your late husband — and it's only a tiny one, if it is a criticism at all — it's that he was sometimes too trusting.'

The late Mr Pargeter's widow nodded in rueful agreement.

'I mean,' Gary went on, 'in many ways he

was too generous-spirited . . .'

'That's true.'

'Too ready to think the best of people . . . an innocent, really, in a wicked world . . .'

Mrs Pargeter wiped a little moisture from the corner of her eye as she nodded again. 'So what you're saying, Gary, is that Stan the Stapler was involved with Julian Embridge?'

The immaculately tailored shoulders in front of her shrugged. 'Can't go as far as saying that. All I can say is it seems odd. Up until Streatham Stan the Stapler done everything for your old man. After Streatham, even though Mr Pargeter offered him lots of jobs, Stan was somehow always unavailable. Well . . .' Another shrug. 'You have to draw your own conclusions, don't you?'

'Yes,' said Mrs Pargeter, drawing hers.

The limousine drew up outside the *Mind Over Fatty Matter* headquarters. Sue Fisher had planted the centre of her empire in the area where she had grown up, the bungaloid sprawl between Newhaven and Beachy Head (offering, in the phrase with which Ellie Fenchurch would begin her Sue Fisher interview, two opposing solutions to weight worries — on the one hand, a ferry to the gastronomic delights of France and, on the other, suicide).

The headquarters was purpose-built — a severely white structure whose award-winning architect appeared to have taken his inspiration from anaemic, elongated Lego bricks. As in the ideal *Mind Over Fatty Matter* body, curves were excluded in favour of angles. The building was a shrine to the goddess of self-denial.

This theme was echoed in the pervasive minimalist *Mind Over Fatty Matter* logo over the entrance, and in the stark black-on-white message on an adjacent board — 'DO BETTER'.

That was typical Sue Fisher philosophy. All her slogans — and she had taken to slogans in rather a big way — contained comparatives. Nothing was allowed to be good in its own right; everything had to be less good than something else. Aspiration — and by definition unfulfilled aspiration — was the dynamo of *Mind Over Fatty Matter*'s success.

'I don't know how long I'll be,' said Mrs Pargeter.

'Don't you worry. I'll wait in the car park.'

'Well, if you're sure . . .'

'That is my job, Mrs Pargeter,' said Gary. 'I mean, someone as important as you, from an organization as important as the one you represent . . . well, they're going to have a chauffeur what waits in the car park, aren't they?'

She giggled. 'Yes, I suppose they are.'

'Who is it you're representing again?'

Mrs Pargeter curbed the giggles and replied demurely, 'Sycamore.'

'Sycamore?'

'It's an acronym.'

'Oh,' said Gary blankly.

'From the letters SICMOR. The Society for the Investigation of Corporate Malpractice by Overselling Representation.'

'Oh yeah?' There was a pause. 'What's that mean then?'

'I've no idea. But it sounds good.'

'Yes. Oh yes,' said Gary, with suitable respect.

Ellie Fenchurch was waiting in the white, cell-like Reception. Nothing so frivolous as a plant was allowed to break up its austerity. The only relief in the stark whiteness of the walls was provided by more black-lettered slogans.

'SELF-IMPROVEMENT IS WITHIN YOURSELF.'

'PRACTICE BRINGS YOU NEARER PERFECTION.'

'GET FURTHER FROM WHAT YOU ARE

— GET CLOSER TO WHAT YOU CAN BE.'

'Who does this cow think she is?' Ellie Fenchurch demanded as Mrs Pargeter greeted her. 'Jesus Christ, Buddah, and Allah all rolled into one?'

'I don't think you're far off the mark.'

The journalist looked at Mrs Pargeter's bright silk suit doubtfully. 'You don't think you should have tried to disguise yourself . . . glasses or something?'

'No. Be fine.'

'But if Sue Fisher saw you at Brotherton Hall . . .'

'Sue Fisher didn't see anyone at Brotherton Hall. She doesn't see other people unless they can be of use to her.'

'Hm. But if your suspicions about her are correct, then she's going to know who you are.'

'If my suspicions *are* correct, I'll be delighted that she knows I'm on to her.'

Ellie Fenchurch nodded. Then she rubbed her thin hands together. 'I'm going to enjoy this.' She flashed a bleak smile at the perfect body behind the barren reception desk. 'We're both here now. Could you see if Ms Fisher is ready for us.'

The girl buzzed through on her switchboard and found out that yes, Ms Fisher was ready for them.

Ellie Fenchurch rose to her full bony height and smoothed down the jacket of her latest designer frippery. 'OK, off we go.' She grinned a vulpine grin. 'Sue Fisher is about to find out what it feels like to be the ingredients of a kebab.'

Chapter Twenty-Two

Sue Fisher's office was as expensively austere as the rest of her headquarters, resembling nothing so much as an operating theatre, an impression which was reinforced by the steel furniture and severely focused spotlights. In place of notices exhorting surgeons to wash their hands, the walls bore further maxims of *Mind Over Fatty Matter* philosophy.

KEEP GOING, BECAUSE FULFIL-MENT IS JUST AROUND THE NEXT CORNER.

THE HORIZON OF PERFECTION IS GETTING CLOSER.

NO ONE CAN MAKE ME BETTER THAN I CAN MAKE MYSELF.

(It was not without irony that this last statement should be displayed at the centre of an empire devoted to marketing products which would make people better.)

Somehow even the chrome-framed photographs of Sue Fisher with various heads of state and celebrities presenting her with awards took on the air of X-rays in this clinical environment.

The medical parallel was completed by the surgical green tunic-suit Sue Fisher was wearing. It was one of the latest range of the company's designs; *Mind Over Fatty Matter* fashions were now diversifying beyond leisurewear. The suit, in common with all *Mind Over Fatty Matter* garments, looked much better on Sue Fisher than it would on any member of the public brainwashed into buying one.

The medical analogy could also have been maintained that morning by saying that the knives were out. Sue Fisher knew full well the kind of journalistic carve-up that was going to be attempted, and she relished the prospect. The light of battle gleamed in her eyes.

It gleamed in Ellie Fenchurch's eyes too. These were two tough women, squaring up to each other. Neither would offer any mercy, or expect any.

Mrs Pargeter relished the confrontation, almost regretting that she could not just sit back to enjoy it as a spectator. She had to remember that she was there to further her investigation.

'Coffee?' asked Sue Fisher, once functional introductions had been completed.

Both her guests said yes, that would be very nice.

'We only serve one kind of coffee here. It's decaffeinated and made of beans from more than one country, all of whose regimes respect human and animal rights. It's made with water containing an amalgam of natural salts and minerals. It's the only one we serve because all other coffees are actually harmful.'

This was a typically uncompromising Sue Fisher sales pitch.

'This coffee wouldn't by any chance be a *Mind Over Fatty Matter* product, would it?' asked Ellie Fenchurch.

'Yes.'

'And the water — is that one of your products too?' asked Mrs Pargeter.

'Yes.'

Now that really *was* marketing — to sell not only the coffee, but also the water to make it with.

'And I suppose it should only be drunk out of *Mind Over Fatty Matter* mugs . . ?'

Sue Fisher was either deliberately or genuinely unaware of any irony in Ellie's tone. 'It does taste better out of them, yes. The mugs are made from a particular kind of clay I came across when I was on a fact-finding mission in The Gambia.'

'Fancy,' said Mrs Pargeter.

'And they're fired by a slow method which approximates very closely to sun-drying.'

'Well, well,' said Mrs Pargeter.

Sue Fisher turned to a device whose chromium frame, bulbous glass, and interwoven tubing continued the medical image, and threw a switch. 'I had this specially designed in Italy. It's based on a model I saw out there, but adapted to work on less electricity . . . you know, for the environment,' she added piously. 'It's the best — and most environment-friendly — coffee machine currently on the market.'

'And that wouldn't by any chance be another *Mind Over Fatty Matter* product, would it?'

'Yes, Ellie. As a general rule, if something's the best on the market, then it *is* a *Mind Over Fatty Matter* product.'

There was something very unEnglish about Sue Fisher's certitude, Mrs Pargeter reflected. No diffidence, none of that fatal English mock-modesty. Nor, of course, any leavening of English humour.

Sue Fisher continued. She was evidently prepared to maintain a monologue on the virtues of herself and her company until interrupted. 'The coffee machine also saves staff time. Everyone here at headquarters has one in their office, whatever their level in the company. Not only is that a convenience, it also avoids all kinds of problems over hierarchy. You'd be surprised how much resentment builds up in the workplace over the simple issue of who is delegated to make the coffee.'

'So here at *Mind Over Fatty Matter* everyone makes their own?'

'Yes.'

'You don't think,' suggested Ellie, gently poisonous, 'that that encourages selfishness and lack of community spirit among your staff . . ?'

Sue Fisher fielded this one expertly. 'No. The point is that everyone has the right to make their own coffee, and also the right to make coffee for anyone else. You'd be surprised at the level of spontaneous coffee-making for others which goes on within the company.' She smiled an invulnerable smile. 'And, incidentally, here at *Mind Over Fatty Matter*, we don't use the word "staff".'

'Oh, what word do you use instead?' asked Ellie Fenchurch sweetly. 'Underlings? Minions? Slaves? Serfs?'

Sue Fisher conceded a humourless laugh. 'No, we're all co-workers.'

Mrs Pargeter, who was enjoying this preliminary sparring, waited keenly for Ellie's response.

'*Co-workers*, eh?' the journalist echoed. 'That sounds very impressive. Very . . . one might almost use the word "idealistic", Sue.'

'Ideals are not something I shy away from, Ellie.'

'Good, good. How refreshing that is to hear in these materialistic times. So . . . here at *Mind Over Fatty Matter*, everyone works for everyone else, is that it?'

'Everyone works for themselves *and* for everyone else. They all feel part of the same process. The goals of personal fulfilment and the company's success become indistinguishable.'

'That's a very clever idea. You mean,' Ellie Fenchurch asked innocently, 'that everyone in the company is on a percentage of the profits?'

For the first time in the interview Sue Fisher coloured. 'No, I don't mean that. That would be impractical.'

'Why?'

'I can assure you we have investigated the possibilities of such an arrangement and I'm afraid it would just be an administrative nightmare.'

'Oh dear. How distressing.'

'But there are plenty of incentive schemes and promotion prospects to make all co-workers feel that they can become part of the company's success.'

'That is a relief.' Ellie Fenchurch smiled

guilelessly. 'So, in this sublimely ordered community, all the co-workers beaver away together for the greater good of *Mind Over Fatty Matter* . . ?'

'If you like,' Sue Fisher replied cautiously.

'Like bees in a hive, maybe . . ? All buzzing about, thinking of each other, seeing where they can help out the other bees . . ?' Sue Fisher did not argue with this analogy. 'All producing as much honey as possible so that they can benefit from the hive's incentive schemes and promotion prospects . . ?'

'Yes.'

Then came the attack. 'And all of them totally subservient to the queen bee?'

Sue Fisher looked — rather appropriately — stung.

Chapter Twenty-Three

Before the guru of *Mind Over Fatty Matter* had time to respond, Ellie Fenchurch pressed on with her offensive. 'But I'm not really here this morning to talk about your management of this company. The fact that you present the place as the ultimate worker's co-operative, whereas in fact it's a despotism — and not even a benign one — is —'

'Just a minute.' The wind had returned to Sue Fisher's sails. 'You print any of that stuff and you'll have my lawyers down on you before your paper hits the streets. *Mind Over Fatty Matter* is run as a co-operative. Every co-worker has the opportunity to fulfil his or her potential —'

'Unless they show too much potential.'

'What do you mean?'

'I mean there's a great list of talented people who used to work with you and who got elbowed out when they started to threaten your dominance of the company. You feel more secure surrounded by yes-men and gofers and actually running the whole show yourself.'

'Look, I thought up *Mind Over Fatty Mat-*

ter. It is my concept.'

'Exactly. And you're very happy to keep it that way, doing all the strategy yourself and having the nuts and bolts work done by others.'

'The art of management is the art of delegation, Ellie.'

'Sure. I've nothing against the way you run this place. It's efficient and it's successful. All I do object to is the fact that you present what is undoubtedly a dictatorship as some kind of benevolent workers' co-operative. I'm not against commercialism, Sue, just hypocrisy.'

'Calling me a hypocrite in print wouldn't do you a lot of good from the legal point of view,' said Sue Fisher coldly.

'Don't worry, I won't do that. I'm not stupid. My interviews always get my point across without breaking the libel laws.'

Given Ellie Fenchurch's track-record in character-assassination, this was a chilling promise, but it didn't slow down Sue Fisher. 'My basic assertion remains that everyone in this company has equal chances to —'

'Equal chances to rise to the level of a glorified secretary, yes. Those who show the talent to go any higher than that pretty soon get cut down to size.'

'That is simply not true. I can —'

'I can give you a few examples, if you like.'
And Ellie Fenchurch started to reel off a list
of women's names.

She was good. Mrs Pargeter felt privileged
to be in the company of such an expert; she
could understand why the late Mr Pargeter
had so valued his Public Relations Officer.

Ellie Fenchurch'd really done her research.
Sue Fisher remonstrated against the first couple of names on the list, but as the catalogue
continued, she grew silent.

'I've been in touch with all of them,' Ellie
concluded smugly. 'And I'm very happy to
include their views as background research to
my interview . . . unless, of course, you'd
rather I didn't.'

Sue Fisher capitulated ungraciously. 'I think
it might be better if you didn't,' she mumbled.

'Good. Fine.' Ellie Fenchurch beamed. 'So
we can get on to the subject I really wanted
to talk to you about . . . which was the reason
why I invited Mrs Pargeter of "Sycamore"
along.'

'All right.' Sue Fisher was quickly regroup-
ing her resources. 'I can assure you I have
no worries on that front. The claims made
for all *Mind Over Fatty Matter* products
have been rigorously researched, and I can assure you that nothing goes on sale in the High

Street until it has undergone every possible testing process.'

'Good. Fine,' Ellie said again. She was deceptively relaxed. Having caught out her opponent once, she felt confident of maintaining the advantage. She drew a printed catalogue out of her handbag. 'Now, in your manifesto —'

'It's not a manifesto,' Sue Fisher contradicted tetchily.

'You could have fooled me. It reads like a manifesto. All the pious principles according to which your company is run. All the promises of how your company will single-handedly sort out the economy, bring hope to the Third World, and save the planet at the same time. For a moment I thought I was right back in the middle of the last election campaign.'

Sue Fisher gave a patronizing smile. 'All right, Ellie. I'm sure you're enjoying your little performance, but what actually is the point you're making?'

'There is a claim in this' — Ellie waved the catalogue — 'propaganda document . . . that you do not market any products which you have not tried and found satisfactory yourself . . .'

'That is true.'

Ellie Fenchurch grinned, luxuriantly in

control of the situation. 'I think I should bring in Mrs Pargeter at this point.'

The lady in question was so entertained by the duel that she would have been quite content to continue just watching it, but she knew where her duty lay and accepted the cue. She opened the folder on her knee and took out a set of papers. 'Yes, we at "Sycamore" are particularly interested in two products. The first is *Mind Over Fatty Matter* Face Polish . . .'

The name had an instant effect. 'That product was never marketed by this company.'

'Ah, but it was *test*-marketed,' said Mrs Pargeter, supremely confident in Ellie Fenchurch's research. 'In the Tyne Tees area. Seven years ago, just after the success of the first *Mind Over Fatty Matter* book, when you were beginning to explore other areas of merchandizing.'

'As I say, the Face Polish campaign was stopped before the product reached the shops.'

'Yes, and why was it stopped?' Mrs Pargeter was beginning to enjoy her role as Prosecuting Counsel. 'Was it because the actual properties of the product did not live up to the claims that were made for it?'

'That was part of the reason.'

'So you mean it didn't' — Mrs Pargeter consulted her report — ' "smooth away wrinkles and restore facial skin to teenage tautness".'

'No. The claims of the manufacturer who wished me to franchise his product proved to be exaggerated,' Sue Fisher replied, shifting the blame away from her own company.

'And I dare say another reason for suppressing Face Polish,' Mrs Pargeter went on coolly, 'was the fact that it brought out the housewives of the Tyne Tees area on whom it was tested . . . in a rather nasty rash.'

'Well —'

' "Dry, flaking skin . . . painful cracking . . . irritation and bleeding . . .' she read on relentlessly.

'Yes, obviously that was one of the reasons why we pulled the product. That's what testing's *for*,' said Sue Fisher defensively. 'It's to see whether there are any unexpected side-effects of a product, and when you do find any . . . well then, obviously, you stop developing that product.'

'I see,' Ellie Fenchurch interposed. 'So Face Polish wasn't actually one of the products you tested yourself?'

'Well, I —'

'Or did you suffer from "dry, flaking skin . . . painful cracking" and —'

'No, no, of course I didn't! I'm only involved in the final stages of testing. Once a

160

product has been tried on a series of —'

'Guinea pigs . . ?' suggested Mrs Pargeter.

'No — volunteers.'

'These'd be human volunteers, would they?'

'Of course they would. It's one of the proud tenets of the *Mind Over Fatty Matter* organization,' Sue Fisher went on devoutly, 'that none of our products have been tested on animals.'

'I see. You'd rather have humans erupting in flaking skin and that sort of —'

'No, no. This is perfectly normal practice. Once a product's been tested on volunteers and proved to have no adverse side-effects, then —'

'But, if it does have adverse side-effects, what happens to the volunteers?'

'Well, I don't know, do I!' Sue Fisher's temper was now extremely short. 'They get paid for their trouble. They *agree* to take the tests, after all. That's what being a volunteer means.'

'Yes. So there are quite a lot of products your company tests that you haven't actually tried out yourself?'

'At the early stages, yes, of course there are. But everything that actually makes it into our catalogue or on to the shelves in the shops, I have tried personally.'

'What about the *Mind Over Fatty Matter* Slimbic . . ?' hazarded Mrs Pargeter.

This product name also stopped Sue Fisher in her tracks. She was distinctly flustered as she retorted, 'That never reached the shops.'

'Oh, but it *did*.' Mrs Pargeter consulted more of Ellie Fenchurch's invaluable research. 'Five years ago. The Slimbic was on sale in the *Mind Over Fatty Matter* shop in Covent Garden. It had no adverse effect on any of the women who bought the product . . . except for the ones who suffered from asthma. They had very serious side effects from eating Slimbics, didn't they? Particularly the one who was unfortunate enough to be pregnant. She —'

'The product was withdrawn immediately after those side effects were known. And the women who suffered were generously compensated.'

'Oh yes,' Ellie Fenchurch agreed. 'The trouble is that someone who's been bought off once is often very ready to be bought off again. Through your lawyers, you "compensated" the women to buy their silence. It only required another payment from my paper for them to end that silence.'

Sue Fisher was furious. 'Chequebook journalism is one of the most contemptible — !'

'I don't think it's any worse than chequebook justice,' the journalist countered evenly.

Mrs Pargeter picked up the attack. 'The funny thing about it is, though' — she turned a page of her research — 'that you've been a long-time asthma-sufferer yourself . . . haven't you, Sue?' There was no reply. 'And yet you didn't suffer any ill-effects from eating Slimbics . . .'

Ellie Fenchurch came in to spell out the point. 'Which would suggest that you never actually tried one.' Still silence. 'Which rather makes nonsense of your claim to have personally tested all *Mind Over Fatty Matter* products which reach the High Street.'

Sue Fisher was broken. 'What is all this? What do you want?' she asked sullenly.

'Very simple,' Ellie replied, crisply efficient. 'You were at Brotherton Hall earlier this week . . .'

'Yes.'

'During which time,' Mrs Pargeter picked up the interrogation, 'you booked in for a Dead Sea Mud Bath on Wednesday morning . . .'

'Yes.'

'Was that with a view to endorsing the treatment as a *Mind Over Fatty Matter* product?'

'There was some thought we might introduce a skin treatment based on the baths, yes.'

'Which was why you were testing them out?'

'Yes. Well, that is to say . . . that's why they were tested out.'

'So you're saying you didn't actually test out the bath yourself?'

'No,' Sue Fisher conceded.

'You weren't in the Brotherton Hall Dead Sea Bath unit last Thursday morning?'

'No, I wasn't. One of my staff tested it out for me.'

In her diminished state, Sue Fisher had even forgotten to call her substitute a 'co-worker'.

Chapter Twenty-Four

'What do you reckon then, Ellie?' asked Mrs Pargeter, as Gary's limousine swept them elegantly towards the good lunch they had promised themselves as a reward for their morning's work.

'I reckon we've got her over a barrel,' the journalist replied, with the assurance that came from having had many of the rich and famous over barrels. 'You're sure you found out everything you needed?'

'For the time being, yes. Sue Fisher definitely wasn't one of the people who overheard me fixing to meet Lindy Galton.'

'No, and her alibi for the time of the murder sounded pretty solid too.'

Mrs Pargeter had had no hesitation about bringing Ellie Fenchurch up to date with all her suspicions. The journalist's investigative skills might be needed further; and, needless to say, with someone trained by the late Mr Pargeter, worries about discretion were entirely inappropriate.

'Yes. I'll get Truffler to confirm that alibi, but I think she's in the clear.'

'On the murder itself. I still think there could be something else suspicious about her involvement with Brotherton Hall . . .'

'Why?'

'Sue Fisher never does anything for nothing. Why was she there in the first place?'

'To make her latest video.'

'Yes, but there are any number of other health spas all over the country where she could have done that. I'm sure she had some reason for choosing Brotherton Hall.'

Recollection of a conversation overheard from Ankle-Deep Arkwright's office came to Mrs Pargeter. 'I did hear her talking to Ank about some kind of testing that he might be doing for her. Or at least she didn't like the word "testing" — she preferred to have it called "trying out".'

'Ah, did she?' Ellie Fenchurch pounced on the detail with relish. It was exactly the kind of pointer that could set her going on a new investigation. 'I'll look into that, Mrs Pargeter.'

'What, for your article?'

The journalist contemplated her long painted fingernails. 'Oh, I don't know whether I'll actually do an article on Sue Fisher.'

'But I thought that was the reason why you cancelled Warren Beatty. I thought Sue

Fisher was going to be your big interview for this Sunday.'

'No.'

'Well, she'd clearly got the impression that she would be.'

Ellie Fenchurch's face took on the post-coital expression of a female praying mantis. 'Yes, I know she did. No, I just set this up to help you out.'

'Well, that's extremely kind, but it does seem a bit of a waste. Do you mean you're never going to publish it?'

'May do, may not. The important thing is that Sue Fisher *thinks* I'm going to publish it — or that I might publish it at some point. She'll always have that threat hanging over her.'

'I see.'

'And rest assured, Mrs Pargeter, if there's anything else you ever want to find out from her, that threat will still be quite sufficient for her to tell you anything she knows.'

'Good.'

Ellie Fenchurch's face glowed as a female praying mantis's might after the first satisfying bite of husband. 'No, she's made a lot of other people sweat. It'll give me a lot of pleasure to let the guru of *Mind Over Fatty Matter* herself sweat for a while.'

★ ★ ★

When Mrs Pargeter returned to Brotherton Hall after lunch, the receptionist handed her an envelope embossed with the health spa's quasi-heraldic logo.

Mrs Pargeter opened it when she reached her room. The contents were word-processed on thick notepaper headed with the same logo.

Dear Mrs Pargeter,

I am so sorry that I'm not able to say goodbye to you in person, but I've been called away on ~~urgent~~ *pressing* business. I do hope that you have enjoyed your stay at Brotherton Hall, and that you will feel welcome to use our facilities again whenever you so wish — and to recommend them to any friends who you think might also enjoy them.

We do offer a range of special discounts and bargain breaks for regular customers, and hope to see you again before long.

Yours sincerely,
P. T. Arkwright
MANAGER

It was an odd letter. She knew that there had been a cooling in her relationship with Ankle-Deep Arkwright, but that did not seem

168

to justify this awkward formality. The contents read like a form letter which might be sent out to any client. It was as if she and Ank had never met.

The only personal touches were the signature and the change of the word 'urgent' to 'pressing'. Both of these were in what looked like Ankle-Deep Arkwright's handwriting.

If that was all he had to say, why had he bothered sending the letter? No communication at all would have been less hurtful than the impersonality of this one.

Her pondering of the anomaly was interrupted by a knock on the door. Kim Thurrock burst in, dressed in yet another *Mind Over Fatty Matter* outfit and full as ever of the joys of Brotherton Hall.

'Thought I saw you come back, Melita. Just popped in to check you're OK.'

'Fine, thanks.'

'Oh, good. Must dash. So much to fit in, what with this being our last day. I'm really determined to be right down for tonight's Nine O'Clock Weigh-In.'

'Good luck.'

'Thanks. I'll do it, don't worry.' Her voice took on a note of religious awe. 'I'm going to get further from what I am, and get closer to what I can be.'

Mrs Pargeter winced at the pervasiveness

of Sue Fisher's cracker-motto philosophy. She wondered whether Kim's hero-worship would have survived the sight of the shifty-looking woman whom Ellie Fenchurch had so discomfited that morning, and decided it probably would. Faith as fervent as that could never be deflected by mere reality.

Kim skipped to the door. 'Can't waste a second. Must keep going.'

'Because "fulfilment is just around the next corner" . . ?' Mrs Pargeter suggested.

But the irony was wasted. 'Yes, exactly,' Kim Thurrock agreed as she opened the door.

'Incidentally, Kim . . . one thing . . .'

'Yes?'

'I heard a rumour of something nasty that happened down in the Dead Sea Mud Baths on Wednesday night . . .'

Kim stopped. 'Oh yes. That poor girl Lindy Galton.'

So news of the murder had not been totally suppressed.

'What exactly happened?' asked Mrs Pargeter ingenuously.

'Well, she had an accident. She was killed, poor kid.'

'Oh.'

'Slipped and banged her head and drowned in the mud.' Kim Thurrock's face became pious 'That's what comes of having unsupervised treatment. It's very important that all exercises and treatments should be conducted under proper supervision.' She quoted a Brotherton Hall tenet. 'See you.'

So, thought Mrs Pargeter, the 'accident' theory of Lindy Galton's death was now official.

And for a moment she almost wished she could believe it.

Chapter Twenty-Five

Gary drove them away from Brotherton Hall the following morning, the Saturday. Kim Thurrock's only regret about the experience was that it had to end. At the Nine O'Clock Weigh-In the previous evening she had achieved her lowest weight since arrival and, though of course complacency would have been politically incorrect according to the Sue Fisher ethic, she did feel quite pleased with herself.

'Oh, the whole time's been so great, Melita. I can't thank you enough for organizing everything. Just been wonderful, hasn't it?'

Mrs Pargeter, whose experience at Brotherton Hall had not been one of unalloyed joy, made some suitably noncommittal response and moved the conversation on. 'How long now till you see Thicko?'

Kim Thurrock grinned nervously. 'Only a week. Next Friday. Oh, I can't wait. And I daren't imagine what state Thicko himself is in. He's a very stable kind of bloke normally, but he always gets funny a month or so before he comes out. I think most of them do. Did you find that your . . ?'

A sharp look from Mrs Pargeter dried up the flow of the sentence and Kim hastily changed the subject. 'Ooh, incidentally, I've got another favour to ask, Melita . . .'

'Yes?'

'Well, I know it's something you don't approve of . . .'

The twinkle was back in the violet eyes as Mrs Pargeter asked, 'Oh really? Now I wonder what you could be talking about?'

'It's this plastic surgery business.'

'Thought it might be.'

'Look, I have actually gone to the extent of making the first appointment with this Mr Littlejohn . . . you know, the free consultation . . .'

'Oh.'

'There, I knew you'd start criticizing me about it.'

'Kim, all I said was "Oh".'

'Yes. Yes. Well, the appointment's for next Tuesday and the thing is . . .'

'You feel nervous about going up to Harley Street on your own and wonder whether I'd mind going along with you for moral support . . ?' Mrs Pargeter suggested.

'Well, yes.'

Kim was rewarded with a warm, comfortable smile. ' 'Course I'll come with you, love.'

'Oh, bless you, Melita.'

'It's this one, isn't it?' asked Gary, as the limousine drew up outside the Thurrocks' modest house in Catford.

For the next hour Mrs Pargeter was caught up in the tornado of Kim Thurrock's re-union with her three daughters, poodles, and mother. There were lots of hugs, and, from the poodles, lots of slobbering. Mrs Pargeter was included in the hugs, but, mercifully, not the slobbering.

The only awkwardness occurred when Kim's mother Mrs Moore produced the cake she had baked to welcome her daughter home. It was a rich chocolate one, filled and crested with cream, and Mrs Moore was very put out when Kim refused a slice. The old lady subscribed to the East End tradition that equated food with love, and was offended to have her affection spurned.

Kim tried to explain, but all her mother could see was filial ingratitude. When Mrs Pargeter left, Kim was still holding out, but with a resolve that was wavering under a heavy barrage of emotional blackmail. Mrs Pargeter didn't think many hours would pass before Kim succumbed to a peace-making slice of cake. The principles of self-denial inculcated by a few days at Brotherton Hall would be no match for the sheer force of Mrs

Moore's personality.

Gary took Mrs Pargeter to Greene's, the discreetly expensive London hotel where she was currently residing. The house Mrs Pargeter was having built was not yet completed; and indeed, given who was building it for her, the prospect of its ever being completed continually receded.

Loyal as ever, Mrs Pargeter had employed one of the late Mr Pargeter's associates to construct the house in which she planned to spend what she rather coyly (and, given her personality, rather inappropriately) called her 'declining years'.

Now it wasn't that Jimmy Jacket — or 'Concrete' as he was known to his intimates — was a bad builder. He was one of the best. Indeed his construction of the hidden basement to the Pargeters' big house in Chigwell stands out as one of the architectural marvels of the late twentieth century; and the tunnel with which he linked Spud-U-Like and the National Westminster Bank in Milton Keynes bears comparison with many more publicly applauded feats of engineering.

But the drawback to employing 'Concrete' Jacket on a project was his availability. He wasn't like some cowboy builders, who're off on another job the minute their employer's back is turned. He had assured Mrs Pargeter that, from the moment he started on her house, he wouldn't take on any other work until its completion.

But the fact had to be faced — 'Concrete' Jacket's attendance record at the site was not good. Maybe he was accident-prone; maybe he just had bad luck; maybe he chose the wrong kind of friends; whatever the reason, he kept having to be away from the job for periods of varying lengths. And, as a result, the building of Mrs Pargeter's dream house tended to progress slowly.

Which was why she moved around a lot, and why she was currently staying at Greene's.

As Gary ushered Mrs Pargeter into the hotel, its manager, Mr Clinton (who, under the soubriquet 'Hedge-clipper' Clinton, had in the past done some useful if unsophisticated work for the late Mr Pargeter) bustled forward in his jacket and pin-striped trousers to fawn tastefully over his most favoured guest.

'We've missed you, my dear Mrs Pargeter. But I do hope that you've had an enjoyable break. Oh, and while I think, there was a message for you to ring a Mr Mason . . .'

'Truffler?'

'I would assume so,' Mr Clinton replied with a discreet wink.

Mrs Pargeter rang through as soon as she was in her room with a tray of coffee and biscuits.

'Mrs Pargeter,' said Truffler with funereal directness, 'how'd you fancy a trip to Cambridge?'

'Cambridge? Have you got something from Jenny Hargreaves' university friends?'

'I would say I very definitely have, Mrs Pargeter. Some very useful pointers they've given me. But I think I've got as much as I'm going to get out of them . . . you know, kids of that age're, like, suspicious of a man snooping into their private affairs.'

'Hm.'

'Whereas I think they'd be much more likely to open up to a woman. Particularly to you, Mrs Pargeter.'

'Yes,' she agreed. 'Yes, they probably would.'

Chapter Twenty-Six

Mrs Pargeter had never had much to do with students. She had left school at sixteen, and though the sum of knowledge accumulated during the early years of her marriage far exceeded that with which most graduates leave university, the process by which she had gained it did not qualify under the traditional definition of formal education.

Nor, though the late Mr Pargeter, philanthropic as ever, had assisted many young people with further education courses (particularly in the fields of law and accountancy), had he introduced many of these aspirants to his wife.

As a result, the word 'student' conjured up for Mrs Pargeter an image of sixties hedonism, of beautiful but scruffy young people drifting around, either in a benign drug and pop music-induced haze, or in a white-heat of determination to take the world apart and reconstitute it from its basic ingredients.

The only real live student she had met in recent years, the painfully idealistic Tom O'Brien, had done something to endorse the second stereotype.

But neither Tom nor Mrs Pargeter's other preconceptions had done much to prepare her for the three young ladies whom she met, through Truffler Mason's introduction, at Jenny Hargreaves' college.

True, all three were dressed scruffily, but it was that neat designer scruffiness affected by all of their generation, a Levi-led conformity as staid as the twin-sets of a few decades earlier. Chloe, Candida, and Chris manifested all the bohemian get-up-and-go of building society cashiers.

Though perhaps they were a bit higher up the social scale than building society cashiers. All their voices were tinged with that distinctive public school quack and clearly none of them had ever for a moment questioned her right to anything.

Mrs Pargeter did not know by what shadings of the truth Truffler had set up the encounter, but the young ladies showed no reluctance in speaking to her about their absent friend. Chloe, who acted as their spokesman, met her at the porter's lodge and took her up to her room. Mrs Pargeter was led into an austere and institutional space, on whose walls soft-focus black-and-white posters of lovers kissing looked asexual and sanitized.

Chris and Candida were summoned from adjacent rooms on the same corridor (where Jenny Hargreaves had also lived) and the four sat down with all the formality of a charity committee.

Mrs Pargeter accepted an offer of tea (when it arrived, it was Earl Grey) and Chloe spelled out the parameters of their meeting. 'I'm afraid we can only give you half an hour.'

'Because, you know,' Candida explained, 'it *is*, like, Saturday, after all, and one does tend to sort of go out Saturday night to —'

'I meant because of work,' said Chloe reprovingly.

'Oh yes, right.'

'We all have exams at the end of this term, right, and must get back to revision as soon as possible.'

'Absolutely,' Candida concurred. 'Sorry.'

'So Jenny's missing important work, being away at the moment . . ?' suggested Mrs Pargeter.

'Oh right, yes, certainly,' Chris agreed. 'With languages the whole four-year course is very intensive. Missing even, like, a couple of days means you have a lot of catching up to do, know what I mean?'

'Are you all doing the same course as Jenny?'

Chris was. Chloe and Candida were doing

English. 'Not that that's any less intensive,' Mrs Pargeter was assured.

'I see. And Jenny wasn't having any trouble with the course, was she? I mean, not finding the work too hard? You don't think there's any chance she's given up because she couldn't cope.'

'Absolutely not,' Chris replied firmly. 'She's very bright, right? Even though she came through the state system.'

'She's quite incredible,' Candida agreed. 'You wouldn't know it to meet her.'

'No,' Chris went on, 'the tutors were really expecting good results from her in this year's exams — and in her degree in two years' time.'

'A model student, eh?'

'Well, in most respects.'

Mrs Pargeter was quick to pounce on Chris's hint. 'In what respects wasn't Jenny a model student?'

'Well . . .'

'It wasn't that she wasn't hard-working, right,' Chloe interposed defensively, 'just that she did one or two things that the authorities wouldn't have approved of.'

Candida added to the defence. 'But she did it from the best of motives, know what I mean. Isn't that right, Chloe?'

'Oh yes, of course. But Jenny was technically breaking university regulations.'

'Right. Not that anyone in authority ever actually found out what she was doing.'

'What are we talking about here?' asked Mrs Pargeter gently.

'Well, it was just . . .' Chloe looked at her doubtfully.

'It's all right. I'm not the kind of person who'd ever shop anyone to the authorities.' (Little did the young ladies know how exemplary, given the information she had from time to time held, Mrs Pargeter's record had been in that respect.)

Chloe was reassured. 'No, no, right, of course you wouldn't. Right . . . well, all Jenny was doing was taking a part-time job during term-time — which you're not supposed to do, right?'

Candida provided more detail. 'She was working as a barmaid five evenings a week — right out of town, so nobody from the university was ever likely to see her, know what I mean, but I suppose it was a risk.'

'And presumably she was just doing that for money?'

'Yes.'

'But just money to supplement her grant?' Mrs Pargeter persisted. 'I mean, she wasn't supporting a drug habit or anything like that?'

Chris snorted with laughter. 'Anyone who can support a drug habit on a student grant and a part-time barmaid's earnings deserves a Queen's Award for Industry. Need a private income for that kind of thing.'

'Absolutely,' Candida agreed.

'Do any of the rest of you have part-time jobs?'

They shook their heads. Colouring slightly, Chloe said, 'No, but then we don't need to. Our parents all help us out. But Jenny's parents . . . well, I gather they haven't got any money — I mean, really absolutely none, right? Or at least, if they have, she never likes to ask them for any . . . isn't that right, Chris?'

Chris nodded. 'Yes. I mean, we all complain about money all the time, right, but we have got some kind of cushion from our parents . . . you know, they give us a bit extra and they'll bail us out if we get absolutely stuck. Jenny hadn't got anything like that. She really was hard-up, know what I mean?'

'Being in the room right next door and seeing a lot of her, I sometimes felt almost guilty about how little she'd got . . . you know, clothes and whatnot. I mean, if I really need something new, right . . . I can just go out and buy it — new frock for a party, whatever — but Jenny really had to make her stuff last.

I mean' — Chris's voice dropped to an awe-struck whisper — 'she even used to mend tights.'

The other two young ladies looked appropriately shocked at this revelation.

'And was Jenny still working as a barmaid right up to the end of last term — well, I mean up to the time she disappeared, anyway?'

'No. That was it, you see,' Chris replied. 'She didn't tell them when she got the job that she was an undergraduate . . . well, obviously . . . you know, she behaved like she was taking it on permanently, right, and when the manager of the pub found out she wasn't going to be around for the vacation, well, she was out on her ear. He wanted someone regular, know what I mean?'

'There just aren't any part-time jobs around these days,' Chloe complained. 'So many real unemployed people looking for work, it's pretty tough for students to get a look in.'

'I haven't even bothered trying,' said Chris plaintively. 'I mean, you know there's going to be absolutely zilch, right . . . so why put yourself through all that heartache?'

'No, right. I mean, last summer vacation,' Candida confided, 'I tried to get something — anything. No, I was really prepared to slum it — muck out stables, be a chambermaid, even a cleaner or something, but, know what I mean, there was nothing. Absolute zilch. Eventually Mummy sent me on a word-processing course just so's I wouldn't be sitting round the house twiddling my thumbs all the time.'

'So you did that right through the vacation, did you?' asked Mrs Pargeter.

'Yes. Well, till we went to Saint Tropez, anyway.'

Mrs Pargeter began to realize some of the social pressures that a girl from Jenny Hargreaves' modest background must have experienced at Cambridge. Or at least at Cambridge surrounded by these three.

Time to move the subject on, though. She was in little doubt that the embryonic charity committee members would restrict her to the half-hour they had promised. 'I believe Jenny had a boyfriend, didn't she . . ?'

The temperature in the room dropped by a good ten degrees.

Chapter Twenty-Seven

Chloe was the first to speak. 'Yes. Yes, she did.'

'Tom O'Brien,' Mrs Pargeter prompted.

'Huh.' The monosyllable left no doubt about Candida's contempt for the young man in question. 'I mean, honestly, you'd think someone like Jenny'd realize that coming to Cambridge was, like, an opportunity for her to meet some men out of her kind of . . . well, some different sort of people, right . . . and she ends up with someone like Tom.'

'What's wrong with him?'

'Well, he's . . . I mean, he comes from a comprehensive . . . he's, like, the kind of person Jenny might have met if she'd never even gone to university — any university, let alone Cambridge.'

'Maybe that was part of his appeal. Maybe that was why she felt relaxed with him.'

'Well, maybe, but what a waste.'

Chloe elucidated, not without vindictiveness. 'I think what Candida's saying is that Tom is a bit . . . common.'

'No, I'm not! I wouldn't use the word "common", anyway.' Candida fell back on a long-held article of faith, certainly learned at her mother's knee. 'Only common people use the word "common", as it happens.'

'Listen, Candida, if you're saying I'm common, you'd better —'

'All I happen to be saying, Chloe, is —'

Mrs Pargeter broke discreetly into this unseemly squabble. 'Girls, please . . .'

Perhaps this phrase brought back to Chloe and Candida the remonstrance of some half-remembered house mistress; certainly it had the effect of silencing them. They turned demurely to Mrs Pargeter.

'What I'd like to know,' she asked, 'is what — apart from his class — you find objectionable about Tom O'Brien?'

'Well, he's got all these ideas . . .' Chloe replied.

'All these notions . . .' Candida agreed.

'All these principles . . .' said Chris with distaste.

'Anything wrong with principles?' asked Mrs Pargeter innocently.

'No, obviously not,' Chris replied. 'Not in their proper place. And not if they're the right principles.'

'What would you say are the right principles?'

Chris's answer dispelled Mrs Pargeter's last illusion of student dissidence. 'Well, keeping things as they are. Protecting property. Law and order. I mean, those are principles worth standing up for.'

'But they're not the ones that Tom stands up for?'

'No. His principles are little short of terrorism.'

'I thought he was into ecology . . . you know, ways of saving the planet . . .'

'Yes, but the methods he reckons are legitimate to actually save the planet' — Chris shook her head in disapproval — 'well, they're absolutely terrifying.'

'Perhaps he believes that extreme problems require extreme solutions.'

'Oh yes, right, I can see the thinking, but they don't have to be *that* extreme. I mean, it's all very well imagining that you can do things to help the Third World, all that stuff, absolutely fine, nothing against it, but you've got to get your priorities sorted out.'

'So what are the proper priorities?' Mrs Pargeter suggested ironically. 'You make the odd gesture to the Third World every now and then, but never forget that charity really begins and ends at home?'

'Exactly,' said Chris, and her two friends nodded agreement, reassured that, in spite of her rather common accent, deep down Mrs Pargeter was their sort of person.

She took advantage of the hiatus to move the investigation on. 'You don't think Tom had anything to do with Jenny's absence, do you?'

'In what way?' asked Chloe.

'Well, that they might have run off together . . ?' Although she knew that that wasn't what had happened, Mrs Pargeter still wanted to find out what the girls thought.

'Oh, no,' Chris and Candida replied in unison.

'No,' Chloe agreed. 'No, we're fairly certain that Jenny went off to work . . . you know, make some money after she lost the pub job.'

'But why would she do that before the end of term?'

'Because that's when the job came up, we assume. And we reckon it must have been something so well paid that, to her mind, it justified the risk of missing a week of term.'

'And do you know any more about what kind of work Jenny might have been doing?'

Chloe and Candida looked interrogatively at Chris, who took up her cue with relish. 'I actually think I've got a pretty good idea of what it was — well, not absolutely what it was, but how she got on to it, know what I mean?'

Mrs Pargeter waited, letting the girl time her own revelation.

'Thing is, being in the room next door to someone, you do live pretty close to them and you know most of what they're up to. I mean, I suppose I tended to go out more than Jenny — you know, like socially — but I still did see quite a lot of her . . .'

'Yes?' Mrs Pargeter prompted patiently.

'And I mean, I know after she lost the barmaid job, she was going through all kinds of newspapers and magazines to, like, look out for other things.'

'And you think you know which magazine she got the job from?'

Chris refused to be hurried. 'Let's say I reckon I've narrowed it down.'

'Ah.'

'Jenny did tend to read some fairly yucky sort of magazines.'

'Oh?'

Chris's face settled into a moue of distaste. 'I mean some fairly subversive stuff . . . like, say, *Private Eye* . . .'

Mrs Pargeter made no comment, but her mind was reeling. The idea that twenty-year-olds in the nineteen-nineties could regard the superannuated *enfant terriblisme* of *Private Eye* as subversive was totally incongruous. What had happened to these girls? Had they sprung middle-aged and blue-rinsed from their mothers' wombs?

'Not that we're wholly against *Private Eye*,' interposed Chloe, perhaps trying to bring a tinge of liberalism into the discussion. 'I mean, some of the covers are sort of quite funny . . . and the odd cartoon . . .'

'But it is all so negative,' Chris argued. 'Knocking things down all the time, not trying to build anything up. I mean, like, you do have to be more positive about things. The government is really trying, doing its best to get this country back on its feet, and I don't think the kind of sniping *Private Eye* does is anything but completely destructive.'

Fascinating though it was to witness this reactionary display, Mrs Pargeter, aware of her time limit, felt she had to move the conversation on. 'So you reckon Jenny went after a job advertised in *Private Eye*, do you?'

'Well, I think so. They do have a lot of small ads, you know.'

'Yes,' Chloe agreed, 'though these days most of the job ones are for people looking for work rather than offering it . . . you know, "Graduate seeks five thousand pounds to change the world, anything considered", that kind of stuff . . .'

'And then of course there are the personal ads . . . the contact ones, know what I mean?'

Candida blushed. 'Some of those are pretty
. . . well, pretty explicit.'

Given more time, Mrs Pargeter would have
loved to pursue this theme and find out if the
three young ladies' attitudes to sex were as
reactionary as their views on everything else,
but it wasn't the moment. 'So, Chris, do you
think you know the actual ad that Jenny answered?'

The girl smiled smugly. 'Got a pretty good
idea.' She reached into her handbag and produced a tattered copy of a recent *Private Eye*.
'I know she was looking at this just a few
days before she went off, and one of the ads
is marked.'

She opened the magazine at the relevant
page and handed it across. Mrs Pargeter
looked at the *Eye Earn* column. In the middle
of the usual encomia for foolproof betting
systems, 'amazing opportunities', and 'superb
home businesses', a few words had been
ringed in red ballpoint.

£5000 FOR FOUR WEEKS' WORK.
NO TRAINING REQUIRED. DE-
TAILS BOX 20335.

'And you're sure that Jenny was the one who
put the ring round it?'

'Of course I am,' Chris replied. 'Saw her

do it.' A funny thought struck her. 'Why? You don't imagine *I*'d have done it, do you? Or Chloe or Candida? Good heavens, can you imagine any of *us* stooping to that kind of thing?'

She let out a quack of laughter, in which her two friends joined. It was the best joke Chris had come up with for some time.

Mrs Pargeter once again felt massive sympathy for the life Jenny Hargreaves must have spent in Cambridge.

Chapter Twenty-Eight

Mrs Pargeter reported her progress to Truffler Mason on the carphone as Gary's limousine sped her smoothly back to Greene's Hotel. 'I mean, I know box numbers are supposed to be a kind of security device, but . . .'

'Mrs Pargeter . . .' Truffler's voice was once again edged with a hint of reproach.

'Yes, I'm sorry. Of course I know you'll be able to find out. Well, needless to say, any connection you can get with Brotherton Hall's going to be terrific. And the sooner the better, obviously . . .'

'Goes without saying, Mrs Pargeter. Incidentally, on the other things you asked me to check out . . .'

'Ank and Dr Potter?'

'Right.' There was a pause before the uncharacteristic admission. 'I'm afraid I haven't made much headway there.'

'Oh dear.'

'It's not for want of trying.' Truffler Mason's voice was drowning under an excess of apology.

'Never occurred to me that it was.'

'No, but . . . Well, I just feel bad. Like I was letting you down.'

'Of course you're not. So what have you got on Ank?'

'Well, really nothing so far — that's what's so bloody annoying. Nothing except the Brotherton Hall party line. "Mr Arkwright is away for a few days." "Do you know where he's gone?" "No, I'm afraid not, sir." "Do you know precisely when he's likely to be back?" "No, I'm afraid not, sir." Right slap up against a brick wall, I am.'

'Sounds like he's deliberately lying low.'

'Yes. Unless he's been laid low,' said Truffler chillingly.

'Hm. What about Stan the Stapler?'

'Same story. "No, I'm afraid Mr Bristow is away for a few days — and no, I'm afraid I don't know when he's likely to be back." Bloody frustrating, I can tell you. I'm not used to not getting a result.'

'Sounds like someone's deliberately stopping you from getting a result.'

'Yeah. That doesn't make it any less frustrating. I'll find a way, don't worry.' But the gloom in Truffler's voice was terminal.

'How about Dr Potter? Anything on him?'

'Well, yes . . .' There was still no hint of satisfaction in his tone. 'Don't like it, though.'

'Nasty secrets, do you mean?'

'No — *no* nasty secrets, that's what I don't like about it. Kind of model history for a medical man. Did all the right training, worked as a GP in England for ten years, then out to Hong Kong. Twelve years out there — good doctor, highly respected professionally, well liked personally — then comes back here and gets the job at Brotherton Hall. I don't like it,' he repeated sepulchrally.

'Why?'

'Because it doesn't seem to tie in with the way he's behaving now, does it? From your encounters with him, you'd hardly call Dr Potter a good doctor, would you? Not one you'd recommend to your friends for his bedside manner?'

'No.'

'Anyway, I'm still pursuing it. Got feelers out with my contacts in Hong Kong — may be able to get some dirt.'

He didn't sound optimistic. But then, come to that, Truffler Mason never *did* sound optimistic.

'Don't worry,' Mrs Pargeter comforted. 'At least now with this box number you've got something positive to investigate.'

'Yes. Yes, that's true.'

Only someone who knew Truffler extremely well would have recognized from his tone that this reminder had actually cheered him up.

Perhaps from frustration at the blocking of his other enquiries or from a need to prove himself (completely unnecessary so far as Mrs Pargeter was concerned), Truffler Mason was back to his brilliant best in investigating the *Private Eye* box number. Indeed, she had just arrived back at Greene's and was only half-way through Hedge-clipper Clinton's fulsome welcome when the girl on Reception announced that a Mr Mason was on the line asking for her.

Mrs Pargeter took the call right there in the foyer.

'I've tracked it down!' Truffler announced with mournful glee. 'Tracked him down, I should say.'

'Brilliant!' said Mrs Pargeter, with a little extra effusiveness to reassure Truffler she attached no blame to him for the blanks he had drawn on his other enquiries. 'Who is he?'

'Would you believe an estate agent?'

'What — so it was an estate agent who was offering the job?'

'Well, yes, but not on his own account, of course. When do estate agents ever do anything on their own account — except present bills? No, he was doing it on behalf of a client.'

'Do you know who the client is?'

'Not yet, but we can get it from him,' Truffler replied with grim confidence.

'And have you found out whether Jenny Hargreaves did actually apply for the job?'

'Not exactly. But the speed with which the geezer clammed up when I mentioned her name makes me pretty certain I'm on to something.'

'Good work, Truffler. What's the next move?'

'I've fixed an appointment to go and see the gentleman tomorrow morning.'

'Me too?'

'You bet, Mrs Pargeter. You can help me nail the bastard.'

'Why, have you got some dirt on him?'

'Not yet,' came the sardonic reply, 'but give me time. You can always get dirt on an estate agent.'

Chapter Twenty-Nine

'And don't worry, Mrs Meredith,' said Keith
Wellstrop of Wellstrop, Ventleigh & Pugh into
the telephone on the Monday morning. 'I'm
well aware of your concern for wildlife and
for the way you've encouraged the pheasants
to breed in the grounds of Ragley House. I
will make it my personal business to ensure
that we find you a purchaser who has just the
same priorities. Yes, yes, of course, Mrs Meredith. I'll call you soon, goodbye.'

He put two fingers down on the buttons
of the telephone and, with a wave to the
couple who'd just come into the office, immediately started dialling another number.
'With you in a moment. One quick call.'

Mrs Pargeter and Truffler Mason smiled acquiescence and pretended interest in the property details on the walls, as the chubby, florid
young man made his connection. 'Oh, hello,
Mr Atkins, it's Keith Wellstrop of Wellstrop,
Ventleigh, and Pugh. Good morning. Look,
new property just come on the books. Wanted
you to be the first to know about it, not telling
anyone else it's on the market for a day or

199

two. Ragley House . . . yes. Well, I thought you'd be particularly interested because it does have excellent pheasant shooting. Yes, good. I'll get the details in the post to you today. Fine. Byee.'

Again he did the fingers-on-the-button-and-instant-redial routine. 'Just one more,' he assured his clients. 'Oh, hello, Mr Carver, it's Keith Wellstrop of Wellstrop, Ventleigh, and Pugh. Good morning. Look, new property just come on the books. Wanted you to be the first to know about it, not telling anyone else it's on the market for a day or two. Ragley House . . . yes. Well, I thought you'd be particularly interested because it does have excellent pheasant shooting. Yes, good. I'll get the details in the post to you today. Fine. Byee.'

Three more identical calls followed before Keith Wellstrop of Wellstrop, Ventleigh & Pugh finally put the receiver back in its cradle and turned to Mrs Pargeter and Truffler with an apologetic spread of his hands. 'So sorry to have kept you. Short-staffed this morning. Flu epidemic on, I gather. So . . . what can I do for you?'

Mrs Pargeter, who had heard nothing about a flu epidemic, did not anticipate the appearance of any staff, let alone Messrs Ventleigh and Pugh. She was convinced that Keith

Wellstrop was reduced by the property slump to running a one-man band.

But she said nothing and, according to their plan, let Truffler initiate the conversation. 'Yes, my name's Mr Mason, this is Mrs Pargeter, we've come about some information.'

'Oh, good. Well, what sort of property are you looking for?'

'It's one specific property we're interested in.'

'What, you saw a Wellstrop, Ventleigh & Pugh board outside and you wanted to — ?'

'No,' Truffler interrupted firmly. 'The property we're interested in is Brotherton Hall.'

Keith Wellstrop of Wellstrop, Ventleigh & Pugh folded his hands smugly over a well-upholstered stomach. 'Well, I'm sorry. I'm afraid that property is not on the market. It's currently being run as a very successful health spa.'

'But did you handle the sale when Brotherton Hall was last on the market?'

'No. We don't deal in properties of that size. Six, seven-bedroom country houses, yes — mansions, no. Now I do have some details here of —'

Truffler cut through all this. 'Do you know any of the management at Brotherton Hall?'

'No. No, I don't.' For the first time suspicion had come into the estate agent's piggy eyes. 'What is this? What do you want?'

'As I said, we want some information.'

'About house purchase?'

'No.'

'Then I don't believe I can help you, Mr, er . . .'

'Oh, I think you can.' From an inside pocket Truffler Mason produced the copy of *Private Eye*, folded open at the small ads. 'I'm interested in this box number, Mr Wellstrop.'

The patches of colour on the estate agent's face spread, conjoining into a uniform purple. 'And what makes you think this has anything to do with me?'

'I know it does,' Truffler replied evenly.

'Well, I'm afraid you're mistaken.' Keith Wellstrop of Wellstrop, Ventleigh & Pugh rose from his chair in a display of authority. 'And if it's not house purchase you're interested in, I do have rather a lot of work to do this morning and —'

Mrs Pargeter came in on her prearranged cue. 'Oh, it is house purchase we're interested in. The purchase of one house in particular. . . .' Keith Wellstrop was momentarily silenced by the intervention, allowing her to continue: 'A house called 17 Doubletrees Lane.'

The purple in the young man's face was

instantly diluted to pink. 'What? I don't know what you're talking about,' he protested feebly.

'Oh, I think you do.' Mrs Pargeter drew a cardboard folder out from under her arm, aware once again of how privileged she was to enjoy the research services of such experts as Ellie Fenchurch and Truffler Mason.

He it was who had provided the data from which she now quoted. 'It was a chain, wasn't it — one of those peculiarly English situations involving six houses, the top one worth half a million and the others getting cheaper and cheaper, right down to 17 Doubletrees Lane, selling for a mere forty-two thousand. And the whole thing was set up, all the purchases sorted out and you in line for very substantial commission when they all went through . . . Not a bad rate of pay for the amount of effort the deals had cost you.'

'I don't think you —'

She overrode him. 'But 17 Doubletrees Lane was the one that threatened the whole deal, wasn't it? Its sale fell through just at the wrong moment. Unless some philanthropist came up with a cash offer, your commission on all the other deals was out the window, wasn't it? Which was why you decided to be that philanthropist. You bought 17 Doubletrees Lane yourself, didn't you?'

By now he'd built up enough head of steam to respond. 'There's nothing wrong with that. It's called chain-breaking. Quite a common practice among estate agents — and one for which many purchasers have reason to be grateful. The agent temporarily buys the house that's causing the problem and breaks up the log-jam. It's not illegal.'

'It is when you use the money other buyers have paid as deposits to fund the purchase.'

Pink again gave way to puce. 'That couldn't happen. The ten per cent deposit paid when an offer's accepted is lodged with the buyer's solicitors until —'

'Are you going to tell me,' asked Truffler Mason quietly, 'that you've never encountered a bent solicitor . . ?'

'I'm sure such people exist,' Keith Wellstrop blustered. 'Maybe I have met one without being aware of —'

'You've met one. You meet one every week at the Rotary Club . . .'

Mrs Pargeter smiled sweetly and consulted her helpful file. 'A gentleman called Hamish McFee.'

Keith Wellstrop of Wellstrop, Ventleigh & Pugh was silent. Pudgy fingers worried at the lapel of his tweed sports jacket.

'We do of course have documentary evidence for all this,' said Truffler Mason.

A last spark of resistance flared briefly. 'But all the deals in the chain went through. None of the vendors or buyers had anything to complain about. Their deposits were all properly paid at the right time.'

'Yes, but it was a close call, wasn't it? Fortunate that just before all those purchasers were due to complete, a deposit was paid on another half-million-pound house . . .'

'And fortunate that the new client's solicitor was also Hamish McFee,' Mrs Pargeter added.

'One of the advantages of operating in a small town, I would imagine,' observed Truffler. 'Everyone uses the same professional people.'

'And you can all meet up every week and scratch each other's backs at the Rotary Club,' Mrs Pargeter concluded.

All sparks of resistance were now dead and cold. 'What do you want from me?' asked Keith Wellstrop of Wellstrop, Ventleigh & Pugh, a deflated Billy Bunter caught stealing from someone else's tuck-box.

Truffler pointed to the *Private Eye*. 'It's back to this box number, Mr Wellstrop. Tell us what we want to know about that, and we'll go away and you'll never hear from us again.'

'You mean that? You won't expose me and

Hamish? I mean, it'd be dreadful. We'd be asked to leave the Rotary Club, apart from —'

'In my view,' said Truffler with a benign smile, 'your having to stay in the Rotary Club will be quite sufficient punishment for any crimes you may have committed.'

'We're not interested in your small-town fiddles,' said Mrs Pargeter. 'We just want to know about this ad. You were the one who put it in *Private Eye* . . ?'

The estate agent nodded.

'And you got all the letters of application . . ?'

Another nod.

'Of which I imagine there were quite a few. So you were used as the perfect front — and stool-pigeon in case things went wrong. And presumably, a lot of people would be keen to have five grand in these inflationary times.'

'Yes. There were a lot.'

'And did you have to sift them through to make a shortlist?'

He shook his head. 'No, I passed them on. I was just a kind of contact point, I didn't have to do anything.'

'Oh, well, you'd had lots of practice in that,' Mrs Pargeter couldn't resist saying. 'Then what happened?'

'I didn't have much to do with it after the

initial bit. The applicants were cut down drastically, a shortlist was made; then half a dozen people were interviewed and a couple were selected and offered contracts for the job . . .'

'Which they accepted?'

The estate agent was back to nods now.

'And do you know if one of the successful candidates was a girl called Jenny Hargreaves?'

There was a hesitation, while he weighed up the possible advantages of his situation. Quickly concluding there weren't any, Keith Wellstrop of Wellstrop, Ventleigh & Pugh nodded.

'Do you know what the work she was contracted for involved?'

'No, I don't. Honest to God, I never asked and I haven't a clue.'

It sounded convincing. Mrs Pargeter and Truffler exchanged brief looks and nodded agreement.

'So . . .' she said, 'only one major question remains . . .'

'Yes,' said Truffler.

'Who was it? Who did you do this little job for?'

The estate agent squirmed awkwardly. 'Look, I only did it for the money. If there was anything wrong, I wasn't aware of it.'

'We asked you who it was,' said Mrs Pargeter implacably.

'Yes.'

'Another fellow Rotarian, was it?' asked Truffler.

This received a further nod. Then came a hesitation, broken by Mrs Pargeter's voice, suddenly steely. *'Who?'*

'It was Percy Arkwright.'

'The Percy Arkwright who runs Brotherton Hall?'

Keith Wellstrop of Wellstrop, Ventleigh & Pugh nodded.

'I never knew his name was Percy.'

Truffler Mason broke the heavy silence in Gary's limousine as it drove them back to Greene's Hotel.

'No,' said Mrs Pargeter. 'Nor did I.'

But she sounded distracted. Truffler knew the reason. It always pained her to find out something bad about one of her late husband's associates. The thought that Ankle-Deep Arkwright had been deceiving her hurt a lot. It brought back the ugly feelings that had followed Mr Pargeter's betrayal by Julian Embridge.

Truffler offered what he knew to be inadequate comfort. 'Always going to be a few bad apples . . .'

'Yes . . .' Mrs Pargeter shook her head in distress. 'It's difficult to readjust your thoughts . . . you know, suddenly to think of someone as bad when you've always liked them and . . .'

'Hm.'

She gathered herself together with an effort. 'Still, it must be done. From now on I have to cast Ank in the role of villain . . .'

' 'Fraid so.'

'And whatever wickedness I can think of realize that he's capable of it.'

'Yup.'

There was a silence. 'Mind you . . .' Mrs Pargeter said ruminatively.

'Hm?'

'I still find it hard to think of him as a member of the Rotary Club.'

Chapter Thirty

'Just a little bit off the bum,' Kim Thurrock pleaded. 'You really can't object to that, Melita.'

'But I don't think there's anything wrong with your bum,' Mrs Pargeter countered. 'I'm not an expert on these matters, but I'd have thought your bum was exactly what the bum of a woman your age should be.'

'Yes, that's just it — "a woman of my age". But I don't want to be "a woman of my age". I want to be the woman Thicko remembers from before I had the girls. I did have a good bum then, though I say it myself.'

'But Thicko's not expecting to see the woman he knew before you had the girls. He's not stupid,' said Mrs Pargeter (though the last point was arguable).

'I just want him to see me at my best.' Then, rather plaintively, Kim voiced her real anxiety. 'I want him still to fancy me.'

'Of course he'll still fancy you, love. Just relax.'

'I just feel, you know, if I can promise him that my bum is, sort of, in hand — that I am, getting something done about it — then he won't worry.'

Mrs Pargeter shook her head, half in pity, half in exasperation. 'He won't worry anyway. Look, Kim, I want you to promise me you won't do anything about this plastic surgery business without talking to Thicko first.'

'Well . . .'

'Promise me.'

'Oh, all right.'

Having made that concession, Kim seemed to relax. She looked out through the crawling traffic of the Euston Road and consulted her fake Rolex. 'Hope we won't be late.'

'We'll be fine,' Mrs Pargeter reassured her. 'Incidentally, is your mother still staying with you?'

'No, thank God. It was hopeless trying to keep on any kind of diet with her around. She kept forcefeeding me cream cakes. Honestly, her generation have just got things so wrong about eating.'

Mrs Pargeter, who was closer to Mrs Moore's generation than her daughter's, smiled comfortably. 'She looks pretty good on it.'

'Yes, but . . .' A light of fanaticism came into Kim's eye. 'Anyway, I'm not going to backslide. I put on a pound or two while

Mum was staying, but I've hardly eaten anything since . . .'

'Kim, you must look after yourself.'

'Of course I do. My body is a shrine, a temple.'

'It's not a temple you seem very relaxed in.'

'That's because I haven't got it perfect yet. But don't worry, I will. I'll do it. On my own. "No one can make me better than I can make myself." You know, Sue Fisher is an inspiration to women all over the world.'

'Oh yes,' said Mrs Pargeter drily.

Mr Littlejohn's house in Harley Street was as unlike a consulting-room as it was possible to be. Anything that might have carried overtones of clinic or hospital had been studiously avoided. The ground-floor rooms were full of dark antique furniture. The windows, discreetly protected by diamond-patterned grilles, were framed by musty bottle-green velvet curtains, which took more of the light than they should have done. On the walls hung Venetian vistas in the style of Canaletto and still lives featuring gracefully dead birds. On mahogany shelves leather-bound books slouched against each other behind dusty glass.

The whole impression was just slightly

tatty, but it was the tattiness of impeccable taste. These are the rooms, everything seemed to say, in which an upper-class English gentleman actually *lives*. And people coming into these rooms were made to feel, not like clients or patients, but like guests.

The image was reinforced by the lady who greeted Kim and Mrs Pargeter. She was a solid English Rose with blond hair swept back behind a velvet band. She wore a navy blue cashmere jumper and a skirt which, without actually being a kilt, gave the impression of a kilt. Navy tights and flat navy shoes with a discreet garnish of brass completed the ensemble. When she went out of doors, she would undoubtedly have sported a Barbour.

To have called her a 'receptionist' or 'secretary' would have demeaned her. She came across as a family friend of Mr Littlejohn, possibly a remote relation, second cousin or something of the sort.

She greeted the new arrivals politely, in a voice which showed she had gone to the same kind of schools as Chloe, Candida, and Chris. 'And you must be Mrs Pargeter.'

'Yes. I came along to give Kim moral support.'

'How very thoughtful. No, I was expecting you actually, because I've just had a call from a Mr Mason, asking if you'd arrived yet.'

'Oh, did he want me to call him?'

'No, he said he was in transit, but he'd call through here again in half an hour or so.'

'I hope that's not a nuisance.'

'No problem at all, Mrs Pargeter. Would you care for a seat?' An elegant but comfortingly dented sofa was indicated. 'And maybe I could get you both a cup of coffee? Mr Littlejohn will be ready to see you in just a moment, Mrs Thurrock.'

They accepted the offer of coffee, and the 'family friend' went off to make the arrangements. Kim looked round rather nervously. 'Bit posh, innit?'

'You'll be fine. Don't worry.'

'Probably means Mr Littlejohn's pretty expensive.'

'I think cosmetic surgery is generally pretty expensive.'

Mrs Pargeter's hopes that this consideration might put her friend off the idea were quickly dashed, as Kim went on, 'Still, Thicko and me've got a bit put away for something really important, so it won't be a problem.'

'But I thought you were down to your last penny. If you'd got some cash, why on earth didn't you spend it to make the last few years a bit more comfortable?'

'Well, er . . .' Kim grinned nervously.

'Thing is, we have got the cash, yes, but we can't really get at it till Thicko comes out. He, like, has to go and get it.'

'You mean it's on deposit?'

'In a manner of speaking, yeah.'

'Where is it?'

'Epping Forest.'

'Ah, I see,' said Mrs Pargeter, understanding completely.

There were some leather magazine folders lying on the table in front of them. Kim picked one up and fingered it nervously. 'Wonder what this is?'

'Probably "Before" and "After" photographs. And pictures of the range of tits and bums available.'

Kim giggled and opened the folder. But Mrs Pargeter had been completely wrong. It contained a copy of *Country Life*. Mr Littlejohn was far too discreet to let his waiting-room give the impression that he was running any kind of commercial business.

The 'family friend' returned with two bone china cups of coffee on a tray, complete with silver cream jug and sugared biscuits on a bone china plate.

'Actually, Mrs Thurrock, Mr Littlejohn is free now. If you'd like to bring your coffee through . . . I'm sure you won't mind waiting, Mrs Pargeter . . .'

'Course not.' Mrs Pargeter picked up a biscuit.

Kim looked flustered. 'Oh, I feel shy going in on my own.' She looked hopefully at her friend.

'I think you'll be better off without me. If I was there, I might actually express an opinion about what you're proposing to do to yourself.'

'Oh, I hadn't thought of that.'

'I think you should be on your own,' said the 'family friend', a Head Girl firmly directing a junior nonswimmer into the pool. 'It is *your* body that's being discussed, after all.'

'Yes, yes, of course.'

With one more look back for reassurance, Kim, the coffee cup rattling in her hand, followed her guide out of the room.

Leaving Mrs Pargeter to that favourite pastime of *Country Life* readers, flicking through the mansions for sale in the front and fantasizing about buying one of them.

The only difference was that, in Mrs Pargeter's case, had she chosen to do so, she could have afforded to make her fantasy reality.

Nearly three-quarters of an hour elapsed before the 'family friend' led Kim Thurrock back, and Mrs Pargeter could see the suppressed excitement in Kim's face. She looked forward to taking her out for a nice leisurely lunch and hearing all about it.

But that indulgence was deferred by the 'family friend' saying, 'Mrs Pargeter, Mr Littlejohn wonders whether it would be possible for him to have a word with you . . ?'

A blink of surprise and then, 'Well, yes, of course. But I must tell you that, having reached my age, if there's anything wrong with my body . . . well, I've learnt to live with it.'

'No, it's not about that.'

I see, thought Mrs Pargeter. It's to find out how serious Kim really is about this plastic surgery business. Or, a cynical thought intruded, Mr Littlejohn wants to know whether I reckon she can pay for it.

The consulting-room into which Mrs Pargeter was ushered maintained the upper-class domestic ambience of the outer rooms. It was all so shabbily elegant that the mere idea of discussing business in such surroundings would have been bad form.

Mr Littlejohn matched his decor perfectly. Whether or not he had used his own skills or those of a fellow practitioner to arrange a little Do-It-Yourself was hard to know, but he did look wonderfully *soigné*. His pin-striped suit, though of exquisite cut, was comfortably crumpled, and the collar of his Turnbull and Asser shirt above regimental tie endearingly frayed. Wings of white in his black hair framed a tanned face from which twinkled two blue eyes, ready to encourage confidences about unsightly physical protuberances (and ready no doubt to ask with unblinking charm for the huge sums the removal of those protuberances would necessitate).

'Hello, Mrs Pargeter, so good to see you. I do hope you don't mind my asking you in.'

The voice, too, had the easy assurance of frayed tweed and three centuries of inbred, unquestioning authority.

'No. No problem at all. You want to talk about Kim.'

'Well, not only about Mrs Thurrock. In fact, Mrs Pargeter —' He was interrupted by the trill of one of the telephones on his desk. 'I'm so sorry. If you'll excuse me . . ?'

He picked up the receiver. 'Littlejohn. What? Oh, yes. Yes, she is.' With an ironical look, he proffered the phone. 'You're very much in demand, it seems, Mrs Pargeter. A Mr Mason on the line for you.'

She took the receiver. 'Thank you. Hello?'

Truffler's voice was urgently doom-laden. 'Mrs Pargeter, I wanted to reach you before you got to Mr Littlejohn's place. I tried Gary's carphone.'

'No, we came in a cab. I thought it would be easier.'

'Well, listen, I've got something new. I've found a connection between Ankle-Deep Arkwright and the geezer you're going to see.'

'What do you mean?'

'This Littlejohn. He and Ank go back a long way. Back to Streatham.'

The word struck its customary ugly reverberation in Mrs Pargeter's mind. 'What?'

'Yes, back to all that Julian Embridge business. Now listen, Mrs Pargeter, just be careful because —'

The line went dead. Mrs Pargeter looked up into the blue eyes of the plastic surgeon.

She could no longer see anything benign in their twinkle.

Chapter Thirty-One

'I got cut off,' said Mrs Pargeter.

Mr Littlejohn smiled archly. 'How appropriate.'

'What do you mean?'

'At a plastic surgeon's. How appropriate that you should be *cut off*.'

'Oh.'

'It was a small joke.'

Very small, thought Mrs Pargeter. And if a joke's function is to defuse an uncomfortable situation, this one had signally failed in its mission. It would have taken more than a feeble joke delivered in impeccable Old Etonian to make Mrs Pargeter feel relaxed at that particular moment.

'Probably Cecilia cut you off inadvertently,' he continued.

The thought that the 'family friend' *would* be called Cecilia passed briefly through Mrs Pargeter's mind, before she moved on to more pressing concerns. 'Why did you ask me to come in here?' she demanded. 'Is it about Kim?'

'No, Mrs Pargeter, it is not, as it happens.

I will have no problem dealing with Mrs Thurrock, as I have dealt with many other women of her age who simply want to turn the clock back a little.'

Mrs Pargeter couldn't help asking whether he thought encouraging such aspirations was a strictly ethical practice.

The plastic surgeon shrugged easily. 'I've never lost any sleep over it. I don't make any promises to my clients that I can't fulfil. I tell them what services I can offer, and it's up to them whether they choose to avail themselves of those services or not. They're not under any pressure.'

'Nonsense. They're under pressure from every magazine they open, every model they see in a television commercial . . .'

'Certainly. But they're not under any pressure from me. It's their choice.'

'And is it a choice many of them regret?'

'I can confidently answer that in the negative, Mrs Pargeter. I have a sheaf of letters from former clients, all saying how grateful they are to me for the improvements I have made to their bodies, and how much better and more confident they feel since their operations. They express a high level of satisfaction.'

'Well, they would, wouldn't they? After they've spent all that money, they're not going to admit it was a stupid idea, are they?'

He bowed his head in gracious acceptance. 'That is certainly a point of view, Mrs Pargeter.'

She knew this discussion of medical ethics was simply playing for time, putting off the moment when Mr Littlejohn revealed what he really wanted from her, so she briskly shifted the subject. 'Well, you know you're never going to enlist me as a client . . .'

'I am well aware of that, certainly. You are one of those rare women I have met who — as I believe a French proverb puts it — "fits her skin".'

'I've certainly never felt uncomfortable in it.'

'I'm sure you haven't.'

But this square dance of pleasantries had to come to an end. 'What do you want, Mr Littlejohn?' she asked bluntly.

Accepting the change of direction, the surgeon packed away his polite smile and assumed a darker expression. 'Mrs Pargeter, the fact is that, although we have never met before, we have many mutual acquaintances.'

'Oh?'

'In particular, we both knew your husband very well.'

'Ah.'

'The late Mr Pargeter was extremely generous to me when I started in my chosen profession. At the time I qualified, I was unfortunately involved in . . . well, let us say a business relationship which made my practising in the traditional way rather difficult . . .'

'What did you do?' she asked with characteristic directness.

He coloured. 'I don't think the specific details are relevant to our current conversation. Suffice it to say that I ended up as a fully qualified plastic surgeon to whom nobody would give a conventional job.'

'And my husband helped you out?'

'Precisely. He was good enough to supply me with premises, with the necessary surgical equipment and — most important of all — with a steady supply of clients who required my services.'

'So you're "Jack the Knife"?'

'Yes, Mrs Pargeter, yes. "Little John" equals "Jack". I suppose there is a kind of neatness about it. I was given the soubriquet when I started working for your late husband, and it kind of stuck. Very happy years they were,' he said nostalgically. 'I got on very well with Mr Pargeter and he introduced me to a remarkable number of clients. Many of them spent a considerable time with me before taking new directions in their careers . . .'

'New directions like South America, the Costa Del Sol, that kind of place . . . ?'

'Your perception is very acute, Mrs Pargeter. Those destinations were particularly popular . . . though many of my clients returned, after an interval, to this country and have had very successful careers here. In fact, one gentleman who at the time I worked on him would, if he'd been spotted, have had to return to prison to complete a twelve-year sentence for aggravated assault, was only a couple of weeks ago elected a Tory MP at a by-election. And . . .'

He was prepared to extend his catalogue of successes, but the look in Mrs Pargeter's eye discouraged him. She was waiting for the 'but', which would tell what had caused a souring of the surgeon's relationship with her late husband.

'But . . .' he began, as anticipated, 'I regret to say that the harmonious state of affairs between myself and the late Mr Pargeter was not destined to continue.' For the first time in the conversation, he looked awkward, his urbanity weakened by indecision. 'I, er . . . the fact is, Mrs Pargeter, your late husband was involved in a business venture in Streatham . . .'

'Oh yes?' she said softly, chilled as ever by the mention of the word.

'We are all guilty of backing wrong horses from time to time, of joining the wrong side and, I'm afraid, in your husband's view, that was what I did after Streatham.'

Mrs Pargeter was not enjoying the direction of the conversation, but said nothing.

'You may have heard of a business associate of your husband called Julian Embridge . . ?'

'I've heard of him.'

'The fact is that Julian Embridge was a very plausible — not to say charismatic — young man.'

'He certainly could be.'

'I was not myself involved in the action at Streatham. My services, by their very nature, tended to be required after the more active part of such a venture was concluded. And when Julian Embridge came to me after Streatham and asked if I would help him, I had no hesitation in saying yes.'

Mrs Pargeter's only response to this bald statement of betrayal was a non-committal 'Oh.'

'At Julian's request, I totally altered his appearance. I transformed him, as the cliché goes, "so that his own mother wouldn't recognize him". And, by doing so, I fear that I incurred your husband's enduring enmity.'

'I would think that was quite likely.'

'Yes. Yes.' Jack the Knife steepled his fingers together and pressed them against his lips.

'So Julian Embridge is probably still around somewhere, totally unrecognizable to his former acquaintances?' Mrs Pargeter suggested.

'Quite possibly.'

'And would you be able to recognize him if you bumped into him?'

'Probably not. I would if I got close enough — I'd recognize my stitchwork — but at a casual glance, assuming he's dyed his hair and all that kind of stuff . . . no, I probably wouldn't know him. Though of course I'd recognize his shape.'

'Oh?'

'That's the most difficult thing to change. I can fiddle around with people's features, I can tighten their buttocks, I can even remove the odd rib to emphasize their waist, but it is very difficult to make a chubby person into a thin person. Julian Embridge, you may recall, was extremely chubby.'

'Yes.'

'That would be hard to change.'

'He could presumably diet.'

'Oh yes, but he couldn't change his basic body type . . . whether he was an endomorph or an ectomorph — you are familiar with these expressions . . ?'

Mrs Pargeter, a lifelong and contented endomorph, nodded.

'So Julian could have starved himself ever
since the surgery, but he would still remain
an endomorph — just a thinner endomorph.
If someone could ever develop a medication
that would change body type . . . well, he'd
clean up. The slimming industry would hail
him as the new Messiah.'

'Hm. So, Jack, have you seen much of Julian Embridge since Streatham?'

The surgeon shook his head. 'Nothing, since
I completed the surgery on him.'

Mrs Pargeter wasn't sure where their interview was leading, though the suspicions she
had on the subject were not encouraging, but
she didn't see any reason to cease investigation. She was in the presence of someone who
knew about her husband's betrayal; she would
jolly well get all the information she could
from him.

'There was another man involved in the
Streatham business . . . dumb bloke called Stan
the Stapler . . .'

Jack the Knife nodded, acknowledging the
name.

'Do you know if he was on Julian Embridge's side?'

'I'm not sure, but the evidence did rather
point in that direction.'

'Hm,' said Mrs Pargeter grimly. Then, deciding that the evil hour could be put off no longer, she looked straight into Jack the Knife's blue eyes and demanded, 'All right, why did you really call me in here?'

He paused before replying and when the words came, they struggled out with difficulty. 'The fact is . . . that I have a feeling of unfinished business . . . between myself and your late husband . . . or now, in his absence, between myself and you. The fact is . . . no one believed me at the time, and I doubt if anyone will believe me now . . . but what I did for Julian Embridge was the result of a ghastly misunderstanding.'

'Oh?'

'When he came to me, I didn't know anything about what'd happened at Streatham. He told me he needed the plastic surgery — under the tight security conditions that I was used to — and he implied that it was to be done with your husband's blessing. Indeed, he even said that your husband was going to pay for my services. That was not an uncommon state of affairs — your husband was a very generous man, Mrs Pargeter — and so I took Julian at his word, and did as he requested.

'It was only after I had completed the surgery — one of the best pieces of work I've ever done, though I say it myself — that I heard the truth. And by then, I'm afraid, your husband was firmly of the impression — and I can't blame him, all the evidence pointed in that direction — that I was one of Julian Embridge's accomplices.

'Worse than that, all of your husband's associates thought I was a traitor and, since he himself was, er, off the scene for a few years, my life was rather under threat. I therefore disappeared for a while, had some cosmetic work done by a friend in Venezuela, and re-appeared in England five years ago to pursue the career in which you now find me.'

'By that time, of course, your husband was dead, and so I never got the opportunity to clear my name with him. Mrs Pargeter . . .' There were tears in Jack the Knife's eyes as he appealed to her. 'I'm going to carry that guilt with me to the end of my days. I loved your husband — everyone who worked for him loved the man — and all I want to say is: If there's ever anything I can do for you, anything at all, please remember — you have only to say the word.'

'Oh. Oh.' Mrs Pargeter beamed. 'Well, that's very sweet of you, Jack.'

'Thank you,' he sobbed in relief. 'But I mean it. I'll only really feel whole when I've done something for you that repays the debt

I feel to your husband.'

'So let me get this right — what makes you feel bad is the fact that my husband never knew you were innocent and never forgave you for the mistake that you inadvertently made with Julian Embridge?'

'That's it, Mrs Pargeter. That's exactly it.'

'And would it help if I was to say that *I* forgive you on my husband's behalf?'

Jack the Knife seized her hands in his and mumbled, tremulous with gratitude, 'Oh, Mrs Pargeter, you've no idea how much that would help!'

Chapter Thirty-Two

Truffler Mason was waiting for her in the foyer when Mrs Pargeter got back to Greene's Hotel, and he had on his face that expression of incurable apathy which meant he was really excited about something.

'What is it?' she asked, instantly alert.

'It's something pretty good,' he said dispiritedly. 'Really very good actually.'

'Come to my room. I'll get some champagne sent up.'

Once they were ensconced in armchairs with full glasses in their hands, Truffler Mason told Mrs Pargeter that he had spent the previous night at Brotherton Hall.

'Not, I take it, as a guest?'

'Er, no. Not exactly. Thing was, I thought I might get some clues as to where Ankle-Deep Arkwright's been hiding himself.'

'Any luck?'

'No, not actually with him, but —'

'What about Stan the Stapler?' After what she'd heard from Jack the Knife, the whereabouts of the oddjob man had suddenly become important.

Truffler Mason looked a little aggrieved at not being able to conduct his narrative at his own pace. 'Well, I did see him, but I got some more important stuff, actually.'

'Yes, I'm sorry. I'm rushing you. You tell me exactly what happened.'

'Well, I got inside about midnight. There was nobody around then.'

'No, there wouldn't be. Early to bed, early to rise is part of the regime.'

'Right.'

'And did you have any problem getting in?' Truffler gave one of his bleak looks which made her regret having asked the question. 'Sorry, sorry. Where did you start looking for Ank?'

'Started in his rooms. He's got a flat at the top of the east wing.'

'I know.'

'But no sign of him there. Doesn't look like he's been home for a few days. I did a quick search of the place, but I couldn't find anything.'

'What were you looking for?'

Again Truffler looked pained at having his narrative rushed.

'Sorry, sorry. Please go on.'

'So, anyway, I thought I'd check out his office downstairs.'

'Behind Reception?'

'Right. Went through all the filing cabinets and that, but I didn't find what I was looking for.'

With difficulty Mrs Pargeter restrained herself from asking once again what he had been looking for.

'But,' Truffler continued, timing his revelation with lugubrious éclat, 'he's got a safe. And it was in the safe.'

'What? What, for Heaven's sake?' Mrs Pargeter demanded in an agony of curiosity.

Truffler was still not to be hurried. 'From the time you brought me into this, I've been looking for something which would indisputably link Ankle-Deep Arkwright with Jenny Hargreaves.'

'And you've found it?'

The investigator nodded. Mrs Pargeter felt a pang of disappointment. Up until that moment she had been nursing the secret hope that some evidence would emerge to clear Ank, that he would be revealed as a victim rather than a perpetrator of whatever evil had been going on. Now, it seemed, that hope was destined to be crushed.

'What did you find?' she asked quietly.

'It's like a contract. There were two of them, actually, signed by different people, both female.' He took a folded paper out of his inside pocket. 'I photocopied the relevant one right there in the office, then put the original back into the safe.'

Mrs Pargeter took the proffered sheet. The agreement contained on it was not elaborate. In fact, it was not so much a contract as a disclaimer. The signatory agreed that, in consideration of the payment of five thousand pounds, she would participate in such dietary, medical, or exercise programmes as were recommended by the representatives of Brotherton Hall Leisure PLC or Lissum Laboratories; that her regime should be conducted under the medical supervision of a physician appointed by the said Brotherton Hall Leisure PLC or Lissum Laboratories; and that she was entering into this agreement entirely of her own free will and that, in the event of any adverse effects being caused by the recommended regimes, the signatory undertook not to make any legal claims against the said Brotherton Hall Leisure PLC or Lissum Laboratories.

'But surely this agreement's not legal,' Mrs Pargeter objected. 'I mean, it could be a licence for them to poison people without any fear of prosecution. That'd never stand up in a court of law.'

'No, I agree it wouldn't. But a legal-sounding document like this could well be enough to frighten into silence an impoverished student, who was breaking college regulations by even agreeing to take part in the programme.'

'Yes,' said Mrs Pargeter, her eye unwillingly drawn to the signature at the bottom of the sheet. 'Jenny Hargreaves' was written in a robust, rounded, slightly childish hand.

The countersignature did not provide any comfort either. 'P. T. Arkwright.' It matched exactly the signature on the impersonal letter of farewell she had received from the Brotherton Hall manager.

'Doesn't seem much doubt that he was involved, does there, Truffler?' Her surmise was confirmed by a mournful shake of his head. 'I hate to think what they made the poor girl take . . .'

'Whatever it was, it doesn't seem to have done her much good.'

'No.' The memory of the body on the trolley was once again vivid. For a moment a rare doubt came into Mrs Pargeter's mind. 'I wonder if this document is enough evidence . . .'

'Enough evidence for what?'

'Well, to prove that Ank was implicated in Jenny's death.'

'And if it was . . ?'

'I suppose we could hand it over to the police and leave them to sort it out.'

'*To the police?*' Truffler echoed in disbelief. 'Are you feeling all right, Mrs Pargeter?'

'Well . . . No, I'm not. I suppose I'm rather put down by the thought of having to go after someone I like. I mean, I really thought Ankle-Deep Arkwright was one of my friends. It's horrible when friends let you down. When I think back to what happened in Streatham . . .'

Truffler Mason quickly shook her out of this uncharacteristic mood. 'This piece of paper isn't worth anything so far as the police are concerned. For a start, they aren't even aware that there's been a murder — assuming that there has. You forget, Mrs Pargeter, that so far as we know nobody has found Jenny Hargreaves' body.'

'That's true.'

'No, we've got to keep investigating Ank until we get the whole picture.'

'Did you go on looking for him at Brotherton Hall after you'd found the contract?'

'Not as things turned out, no. Actually, I'm pretty convinced he isn't there. I was going to check over the whole place — particularly the basement level . . .'

'Down by the Dead Sea Mud Baths?'

'Right. There's a whole network of other cellars down there.'

'Ideal places for someone to hide?'

'Or for someone to be hidden.'

236

'What do you mean?'

'I'm pretty sure that they may have some other people locked down there.'

'People like Jenny? Who they're testing drugs on or . . ?'

He nodded. 'That's what I reckon. Remember — I found another contract apart from Jenny's. There may be even more we don't know about.'

'Yes,' said Mrs Pargeter grimly.

'I went down to the cellars last night.'

'And did you find anyone?' she asked breathlessly.

'No. I was . . . how shall I put it . . . interrupted.'

'Someone saw you?'

'Not quite. Close shave, though. I was down working on the cellar door with a picklock when I heard footsteps approaching. I hid back in the shadows and someone passed me and went through into the cellar.'

'Who?'

'Stan the Stapler.'

'Ah,' said Mrs Pargeter, another residual chance of thinking the best of someone shattered. 'So he's back. You're sure he didn't see you?'

'Positive. But I thought it was too much of a risk to stay if he was wandering round the place, so I scarpered. One interesting thing, though . . .'

'What?'

'Stan was carrying a tray with covered dishes on it . . .'

'Oh.'

'Suggesting that there might be someone down there.'

'Hiding?'

'Possible, Mrs Pargeter. Though I think the other possibility is more likely.'

'Being kept down there against their will, you mean?'

'That's exactly what I mean, yes.' A new thought came to him. 'Oh, just remembered — there's one other important thing I found out, Mrs Pargeter.'

'What?'

'Lissum Laboratories.'

'Yes?'

'I spent this morning investigating Lissum Laboratories, finding out who owns them. It wasn't easy. They're held through a lot of different companies — in fact, I think there's little doubt that an elaborate chain has been set up deliberately to obscure who the real owner is.'

'But I assume you managed to work your way through that chain?'

He nodded modestly. 'Yes.'

'So who is the ultimate owner?'

'*Mind Over Fatty Matter*. In other words, Sue Fisher.'

'Ah,' said Mrs Pargeter. 'Now that *is* interesting.'

Chapter Thirty-Three

'I cannot think of anything I would enjoy more,' said Ellie Fenchurch when Mrs Pargeter tentatively made the proposal. 'I'd love to see that cow squirm.'

The journalist dropped everything the minute Mrs Pargeter's call came through. She deferred the long-set-up telephone chat with Madonna and cancelled the interview with J. D. Salinger, who was at the time travelling incognito in England. Ellie Fenchurch had never had any doubt where her first loyalty lay. When she thought of all that the late Mr Pargeter had done for her . . .

Gary once again delivered them in front of the blanched *Mind Over Fatty Matter* headquarters. There was no delay; they were ushered immediately into the presence of the boss (no doubt known within the company as the 'senior co-worker'). Whatever Ellie had said on the phone when arranging the encounter, it had worked. Sue Fisher looked defensive, a rare posture for her, and one that she clearly wasn't enjoying.

She began with professional coolness, however, as if the meeting was nothing out of the ordinary. 'I gather there were a few details you wanted to check up on for your profile, *Ellie.*' She invested the name with poisonous gentility.

The journalist went straight for the throat. 'I don't think you'd want the details I'm after to appear on any profile, *Sue.*'

'What are you talking about?'

'Lissum Laboratories.'

They could see the name's impact on Sue Fisher's face in the split-second before she covered up. 'I'm afraid I still don't know what you're talking about.'

'Don't bother with all that,' Ellie Fenchurch snarled. 'We've traced the ownership. There's no question that you own Lissum Laboratories.'

'Well, what if I do?'

'There are things going on there that don't fit in very well with the squeaky-clean image of *Mind Over Fatty Matter.* Certain experiments are conducted at Lissum Laboratories that don't accord with the high-flown ethical principles you keep banging on about, Sue — or with those self-righteous little slogans which are plastered all over your products.'

'I'm sure that's not the case. I can guarantee that nothing being developed at Lissum Laboratories is tested on animals.'

'No,' Ellie agreed.

'Well then, I don't see —'

'But some of it's tested on *humans*.' Sue Fisher seemed unable to think of an appropriate response to this, so Ellie went on, 'Now, I know in this country, that's very much a secondary consideration, way down in the scale of things. So long as beagles aren't being forced to chain-smoke and little pussycats aren't being injected with cancer cells, most people aren't that fussed about what happens to mere human beings. Mind you, I think if details of what has gone on under the Lissum Laboratories umbrella were published, you still might get a bit of reaction.'

Sue Fisher remained silent. Mrs Pargeter watched her closely. The woman was under attack, but by no means defeated. The formidable will that had built up the *Mind Over Fatty Matter* empire was not easily broken.

'I have very good lawyers,' Sue Fisher announced eventually. 'If you try to publish any such allegations, we'll take your paper for millions.'

'Even if I have detailed research to back up what I'm writing . . ?'

Sue Fisher grinned, sensing a recovery of control. 'I said they were *very good* lawyers. They'll have injunctions out before your article hits the streets. And even if something did somehow creep out in print, they'd get you.'

'Even if what I'm printing happens to be the truth?'

Sue Fisher, now considerably more relaxed, laughed out loud. 'I didn't think you were that naïve, Ellie. We're talking about a libel case here — the truth doesn't come into it. My lawyers always get the results they're paid to get.'

The journalist nodded, accepting the inevitability of this, and Sue Fisher pressed forward her advantage. 'I would also like to point out that I serve on a government environmental committee with the owner of your newspaper, Lord Barsleigh. And that *Mind Over Fatty Matter* has put a great deal of money in the paper's Save the Rainforest Initiative. As you know, it's an issue about which Lord Barsleigh is particularly concerned — as anyone would be who is desperate to divert public attention from the number of trees which are cut down daily to provide the material on which his paper is printed.'

'What are you saying?'

'I'm saying if I were you, I wouldn't push my luck, *Ellie*.' Again the name was infused with saccharine venom. 'Lord Barsleigh might well be more willing to sacrifice one journalist than the *Mind Over Fatty Matter* investment.'

'I take your point.'

Sue Fisher stretched out her perfect body preeningly in her chair. 'So I don't really think what you're talking about poses that much of a threat to me or my company, do you?'

Ellie Fenchurch conceded the point. 'No, publicity about a few dodgy experiments in some far-flung department of your empire is hardly going to bring the whole edifice tumbling down, is it?'

'I'm so glad you understand that.'

'Oh yes. I mean, after all, what could I do — if I was lucky, find a couple of women who'd had an allergic reaction to some cosmetic they tested for Lissum Laboratories . . ? And probably by the time I found them, the rash would have faded . . . Just be their word against yours, wouldn't it? And who's going to believe some disgruntled little housewife against the might of an institution as clean and as green as *Mind Over Fatty Matter* . . ?'

'Precisely,' said Sue Fisher, her confidence flooding back.

'But it'd be rather different if someone were to *die* from the effects of some product they'd tested for you, wouldn't it?'

If Ellie had been expecting a reaction of appalled horror, she must have been disappointed. All she got was a light laugh and 'Yes, if that had happened, the situation would be very different. Since it hasn't happened, I don't see that I really have a problem.'

To Mrs Pargeter, alert for signs of lying, the reaction appeared completely genuine. Sue Fisher did not know about the death which had taken place at Brotherton Hall, or if she did know of it she had no suspicions of its possible connection with drug-testing.

'It *has* happened . . .' said Ellie Fenchurch quietly.

'What!' The shock in this monosyllable confirmed Mrs Pargeter's conclusions.

'And a product developed at Lissum Laboratories was definitely implicated.'

The confidence in Ellie's tone belied her lack of proof, but it still had the effect of draining her opponent's confidence. Sue Fisher looked deeply shaken as she asked, 'What are you proposing to do about it?'

'Well . . . I'm not a vindictive person,' Ellie lied genially. 'I think we should come to an arrangement.'

'What kind of an arrangement?'

'An arrangement of mutual benefit. I agree not to publish any of the material I have on you — indeed, to keep *Mind Over Fatty Matter*'s name out of any investigation that might emerge . . . in exchange for certain information.'

'Why should I give you further information? You aren't well known in journalistic circles for your discretion. How do I know you won't just print anything I tell you, in addition to the material you've already got?'

'Because I want to keep my job. You're right — if Lord Barsleigh was given the choice of losing me or losing the money you're putting into his righteous environmental endeavour . . . I'd be out, no question. My feet wouldn't touch the ground. On the other hand, if I was out . . . I'd have nothing to lose, so I'd get my findings published somewhere else — some environmental publication maybe . . . What's the name of that one that's always banging on about all the wonderful stuff your company's done to save the planet . . ?'

Sue Fisher recognized the potency of the threat. 'You're saying that to keep you quiet I have to give you more potentially damaging information?'

'That's it.'

'But I could ruin you — don't you realise?'

'And I could ruin you. But neither of us wants to do that. In fact, it's in both of our interests not to do that.'

Sue Fisher nodded as she thought through

the implications. She reached a decision. 'All right. What do you want to know?'

'I want a list of all the products currently in development and testing at Lissum Laboratories.'

Sue Fisher catalogued the required information in an unemotional voice. Ellie wrote the details down in shorthand.

There were few surprises. A set of variations on the theme of cosmetics and shampoos.

Only one item didn't fit. It was a drug treatment for slimming. Not only did it act as an appetite-suppressant, it also offered the possibility of changing the body's basic metabolism. Tests were at an early stage, but the treatment showed promising signs that it might be able to change an endomorph into an ectomorph.

Back at Greene's that evening Mrs Pargeter filled Truffler in on the day's findings over more champagne.

'That could be quite an important product,' he announced mournfully after she had finished.

'I'll say. It's the Holy Grail of the slimming industry. Anyone who could produce a safe drug that has that effect would just clean up.'

'Yes, though it seems they haven't yet.'

'Haven't what?'

'Produced a *safe* drug.'

'No.' Mrs Pargeter once again was sobered by the recollection of the girl's body on its trolley. She crowded the image out with new thoughts. 'So it seems as if Ank is in it right up to his neck this time.'

'Looks that way,' Truffler agreed in deepest sympathy.

'He put in the small ad, interviewed the students, got them to sign that spurious contract, and then . . . what? Do you reckon he actually administered the drug to them?'

'Maybe he delegated that bit, Mrs Pargeter.'

'Hm?'

'Remember, I saw Stan the Stapler taking a tray down to the cellars at Brotherton Hall. There were covers over the dishes. I don't know what was underneath those covers.'

'No. No . . . Good Heavens, Truffler — are you suggesting that there might still be another guinea pig suffering the same appalling treatment at Brotherton Hall?'

'There were two contracts, weren't there?'

'Yes. We must get back there, Truffler!'

'That's rather the conclusion I was coming towards, Mrs Pargeter.'

'We must go there straight away! Maybe there's another young life at risk. Come on, this is pressing business.'

Truffler let out a mirthless, bitter laugh. But then even his happiest laughs were mirthless and bitter. 'Does me good to hear you say that, Mrs Pargeter.'

'What?'

' "Pressing business." That was one of your husband's favourite expressions. You must have picked it up from him.'

'Suppose I must,' said Mrs Pargeter, busying herself with getting handbag and coat together.

'And of course we all — you know, the blokes who worked with Mr Pargeter — we all used that expression as a danger code.'

'What do you mean?' she asked, abstracted.

'Well, if you was in trouble and you had to get a message to someone else in the organization . . . if you used the expression "pressing business", they'd know what you meant.'

Mrs Pargeter froze, then suddenly started scrabbling through the contents of her handbag.

'What's up?'

'I'm looking for a letter, Truffler.' She located it and tugged the paper from its envelope. 'This is what Ankle-Deep Arkwright left for me at Brotherton Hall. I thought it was just a form letter, but — look!'

She pointed to the line where 'I've been

called away on urgent business' had been amended in longhand to 'pressing business'.

Truffler Mason was suddenly pale. 'My God!' he breathed. 'We must get down to Brotherton Hall as quickly as possible!'

Chapter Thirty-Four

It was not a suitable occasion to use Gary's services. Secrecy was to be the keynote that night, and so no gleaming limousine drew up at the main doors of Brotherton Hall.

Truffler Mason parked his car in a quiet road outside the perimeter and led the way through a small gate into a wooded area through which the jogging track wound. But they encountered no ardent keep-fitters forcing their bodies to another circuit at that time of night. The 'early to bed, early to rise' regime guaranteed that all the health spa's guests were safely tucked up in their beds dreaming guilty dreams of cream cakes and blissful lethargy.

But then it wasn't the guests who worried Truffler and Mrs Pargeter.

They crept from the woods across a small area of lawn to the protection of the ornamental garden in which she had seen Stan the Stapler dragging the pond less than two weeks before. Hugging the shadow of a hedge, they sidled up to the building, homing in on small delivery hatch Truffler had

251

located on his previous visit.

This was locked, but his skills with a pick-lock were such that it opened as easily and quickly as if he'd had a key. He slid inside first to check the coast was clear, then ushered in Mrs Pargeter. She eased her considerable bulk gracefully through the narrow aperture, and was once again inside Brotherton Hall.

They had landed in a storeroom, stacked high with crates of mineral water. Its door to the rest of the house was locked, but this too only delayed Truffler a matter of seconds.

They found themselves in a narrow passage, dimly lit like the rest of Brotherton Hall, but carpeted in an ugly, rough cord which showed them to be in the staff rather than guest quarters.

'I think we're on a sort of mezzanine level,' he murmured. 'We can get to the cellars this way.'

Moving cautiously, with a noiselessness that belied his huge frame, Truffler led Mrs Pargeter along the sombre corridor, through a couple of doors from which shreds of green baize still hung, until they confronted a heavily studded door in oak.

'This must be the way down,' Truffler breathed in Mrs Pargeter's ear.

She looked dubiously at the huge keyhole in its metal boxed casing. 'Take more than a picklock to open that. You'll need a hammer-drill or gelignite.'

'Let's see.' Truffler leant forward and grasped the doorhandle. Tensing himself for the effort, he tried to turn the heavy metal ring.

It gave instantly and the door swung inward. He turned to Mrs Pargeter and, with a defeated wink, whispered, 'An old trick, but it sometimes works — particularly when the door hasn't been locked.'

It opened on to stone steps. There was no light ahead and chill, stale mausoleum air breathed against their faces.

'Better close the door, Mrs Pargeter. Don't want to leave more calling-cards than we have to.'

Truffler produced a pencil-torch from his inside pocket and directed its beam towards Mrs Pargeter's elegantly shod feet on the worn stone steps. 'Mind how you go,' he said and gently pulled the oak door to behind them.

The network of cellars outlined in a fragmentary way by the tiny torchbeam was surprisingly extensive, running under most of Brotherton Hall's ground-floor area. Side rooms spread off like fishbones from the central spine of the passage they walked along. All had been used for storage at some period.

In some the dusty detritus had laid undisturbed for centuries, but in others superseded models of exercise bicycles and other training impedimenta bespoke more recent use.

Their progress was slow, as the torchbeam probed each dark space in search of human signs, but suddenly Truffler froze and tapped Mrs Pargeter on the shoulder to still her too. They listened intently and both heard a tiny scrape of metal on metal.

He tapped her shoulder again and they moved towards the source of the sound. It emanated from a room whose relative lack of dust showed that it had been in recent use. As the beam of Truffler's torch raked the walls, the scraping sound speeded up, almost to a frenetic level, as if someone or something was trying to escape its bonds.

The torch found the source of the sound first, framing a wrist handcuffed to a rusty pipe. Its movements grew even more panicked, straining hopelessly to escape.

As the light moved up the body, its head was suddenly averted and a muffled, fearing groaning joined the metallic scrape.

But Mrs Pargeter had recognized the suit. She rushed forward to put a reassuring hand on the man's shoulder. 'It's all right, Ank,' she said. 'It's Truffler and me — Mrs Pargeter. We'll get you out of this.'

The face that turned in gratitude to hers was bisected by a thick strip of sticking plaster. Mrs Pargeter reached tentatively towards the corner and Ankle-Deep Arkwright's eyes encouraged her to rip it off.

This she did, in one quick, agonizing movement.

'Oh, thank God,' he groaned. 'Thank God. I never thought I was going to get out of here.'

'Don't worry. You can do the handcuffs, can't you, Truffler?'

The big man nodded and leaned forward, feeling in his pocket for another set of picklocks. He passed the torch to Mrs Pargeter, who needed no telling where to point it.

'Hm, bracelets like these are always tricky,' he said, as he riffled through the fan of tiny wires. 'Don't worry, though, Ank. Soon be free.'

'Be as quick as you can. Won't be long before they're back.'

'That's the baby,' Truffler murmured in relief as he felt a wire engage in the handcuff's lock.

But just as he clicked it home, they all heard a loud clang from the doorway and turned to face a sudden blaze of powerful light.

Though the torch was focused on them, light spilled out behind, and, distorted against the low, uneven walls of the cellar, they could see, grotesquely amplified, the shadow outline of the man who carried it.

Stan the Stapler.

Chapter Thirty-Five

They stood frozen like rabbits in the head-lights of an oncoming Land-Rover. As her eyes accommodated the glare, Mrs Pargeter saw that in his other hand Stan the Stapler held a snub-nosed automatic pistol.

She was astonished at the speed with which Truffler Mason moved. Projecting himself suddenly forward, he curled over into a ball, somersaulted, and scissored his legs around Stan the Stapler's as his body straightened out. The torch went flying from Stan's hand and Truffler reached up to seize the wrist that held the gun.

A brief struggle ensued, before the weapon was wrenched free and sent scuttering away into the passage. Then Stan the Stapler was lifted high, immobilized from behind by the lock Truffler had on his arms. The thug gurgled in a grotesque parody of terrified speech.

'Well done, Truffler!' Mrs Pargeter congratulated in an excited whisper. 'Brilliant!'

But Ankle-Deep Arkwright didn't seem to

agree. 'Let him go, you fool. He's on our side.'

'What?'

'Stan's been helping me. They were going to let me starve down here. He's the one who's been bringing me food.'

Truffler wasn't convinced. He didn't release his hold. 'What do you mean?'

'Yes,' Mrs Pargeter chipped in, 'what *do* you mean? Stan hasn't behaved in a very friendly way to me. There's a long history there, anyway, between him and Mr Pargeter. Going right back to what happened in Streatham.'

Stan the Stapler's gurgles redoubled at the mention of the word, but Ankle-Deep Arkwright protested, 'No, people got him all wrong over Streatham. Because Stan can't talk, he never got the chance to explain what really happened. Yes, he thought Julian Embridge was OK — a lot of us did, Jack the Knife and all — and by the time we realized he was a bad 'un, your husband'd already been sent down. Led to a lot of misunderstandings for a lot of people, that did.'

'Then why was Stan the Stapler so surly with me from the moment I arrived here?'

'Because, Mrs P., he was afraid of you. He thought you thought the worst of him — he thought you believed all that stuff about him

258

helping Julian Embridge shop your old man. He was embarrassed, like, that's all.'

'But if he's on your side, Ank, why on earth didn't he just set you free?'

'Because he's afraid of what they'd do to him. Anyway, even if we got away, we wouldn't get far. They'd either deal with us themselves or shop us to the police. We've both got records as long as a gorilla's arm, enough to get us put away for a two-figure stretch if anyone grassed.'

'But, for goodness' sake, who are *they*?' Mrs Pargeter pleaded.

The answer to her question came immediately, though not in the form she would have chosen. It was supplied visually, as two men burst in through the doorway. One brandished a baseball bat, the other an automatic weapon as snub-nosed as Stan the Stapler's but even more bulky.

The baseball bat crashed down on the back of Truffler's skull. He collapsed like a handless glove-puppet, releasing Stan, who turned, pale with fear, to face the assailants, then backed away with his hands up to join Mrs Pargeter and Ankle-Deep Arkwright.

One of the men switched on the light and the room was flooded with searing whiteness. Mrs Pargeter blinked a couple of times and then, with horror, recognized the two men who had wheeled away Jenny Hargreaves' body.

She knew now that they weren't real ambulance men. She knew also that they had disposed of Jenny's body in some nameless way. She didn't feel encouraged about the way they were likely to treat people who got in their way.

Nor did their first words inspire in her any greater confidence.

'Shall we just shoot them straight away?' asked the first ambulance man.

'Yes. We'll have to do it some time. Let's get it over with.'

The one with the gun gestured the three of them to back against the wall, then looked down at the unconscious Truffler Mason.

'Better sort out this one first,' he growled and brought the snout of his weapon down against Truffler's unprotected temple.

'Stop!' Mrs Pargeter prepared to scream, but was amazed to hear the word spoken before she had even drawn breath.

The sound came from the doorway where, armed with a machine-gun, stood Dr Potter.

Chapter Thirty-Six

The frame of the doorway emphasized the disproportion of Dr Potter's body. His thin legs looked too long, his thin arms too short, his head somehow shrunken above bony shoulders.

But, his appearance notwithstanding, there was no doubting his authority. The two bulky ambulance men positively cowered away from him.

'Throw the gun on to the floor,' he snapped, and the order was instantly obeyed. 'God, what kind of animals are you, if you imagine shooting people in cold blood is going to achieve anything? There is enough mindless violence in the world already without adding to it.'

Mrs Pargeter was surprised to hear these sentiments coming from a man to whom she had taken such instant dislike, but they were none the less welcome. She had realized when the gun was at Truffler Mason's temple how much she loved him — how much indeed she loved all her friends, and how little she wanted to be separated from them, either by their death or her own. At this latest reprieve, the joy of living, the sheer delight of being alive, surged through her.

First things first, she rushed forward to the recumbent Truffler. He was unconscious, but the evenness of his breathing offered hope of no permanent damage. She looked up at their Saviour.

'Dr Potter!' she cried. 'Thank you. That was a very close shave.'

'I agree,' he said without emotion. 'It's dreadful to think how much destruction these two ruffians could have caused.'

'Yes, yes,' Mrs Pargeter agreed enthusiastically. 'And, Ank, isn't it terrific that . . ?'

But something she saw in the Brotherton Hall manager's eye dried up the words on her tongue. She looked quickly at Dr Potter, then back to Ankle-Deep Arkwright.

He nodded grimly. 'Dr Potter's the one who imprisoned me down here. The two goons are paid heavies. They just do as they're told.'

'But . . .' Mrs Pargeter looked up in bewilderment.

The doctor, very coolly and efficiently, explained it to her. 'Yes. A lot of people just do as they're told. It's wonderful what most people can be persuaded to do when you've got a bit of dirt on them.'

Mrs Pargeter, whose investigative methods

had frequently borne out the truth of this statement, nodded.

'And I have a lot of dirt on a lot of people,' Dr Potter continued. 'A surprising amount of dirt. I had enough on Mr Arkwright when I returned from Hong Kong to ensure that he would give me the job here, and allow me all of Brotherton Hall's resources for my work. I had enough on Stan and — he gestured contemptuously towards the ambulance men — '*these two* to command their unquestioning obedience. And, if I chose to use it, I'd have enough to get Truffler Mason put away for a very long time.'

'You haven't got anything on me,' said Mrs Pargeter defiantly.

'No, but then I don't need anything on you. You're just a nuisance, a minor irritation. There's nothing you can do to help me in my work.'

'And what is that work?'

The thin face crackled into a thin smile and the mud-coloured eyes produced what in any other eyes would have been a twinkle. 'I am a research scientist, Mrs Pargeter. Rather a good one, as it happens. The trouble is, the kind of research I do might not be sanctioned in a traditional pharmaceutical company. Such institutions tend to be very old-fashioned — though I can guarantee that, once my current product has reached its final form, all the drug companies will instantly copy it.'

'What is the product?'

'Ah, Mrs Pargeter, ever ready with the direct question. My product is something on which I have been working for many years. I first developed it for . . . well, I don't think that's really relevant at the moment. Suffice it to say that the product is very nearly in its final form. And when it has reached that form, it will make me a very rich man indeed.'

'It's for slimming, isn't it? To change a body's basic metabolism, to turn a naturally fat person into an unnaturally thin person?'

He nodded acknowledgement of her investigative expertise. 'Very good, Mrs Pargeter. That is exactly what it is.'

'And when you get it right, you're going to market it through Sue Fisher's *Mind Over Fatty Matter* outlets.'

'I am indeed. When you have the best product in the world, you go for the best distribution system. Sue Fisher is very excited about the drug.'

'Even though it has been tested on student guinea pigs and caused the death of at least one of them?'

Dr Potter shrugged. 'The advances of science have never been achieved without casualties, Mrs Pargeter.'

Suddenly in her head were the words she had overheard on her first night at Brotherton Hall. 'But there's nothing you can do about it. They're going to kill me, and nobody can stop them.'

The girl had not been talking about people going to kill her — not directly at least. She had been talking about the drugs she had been paid to take, drugs whose deleterious effects were by then too far advanced to be halted.

Mrs Pargeter looked contemptuously at Dr Potter. 'You just don't care, do you? You don't care about the girl who died.'

He shrugged again. 'She took a risk. She knew she was taking a risk. And she was extremely well paid for the risk she took.'

'But what about her parents?'

'She said she had no parents. I was extremely careful only to take on applicants who had no close family.'

'So that if anything went wrong, no one would come looking for them?'

'Exactly.'

'The girl did have parents.'

'If she lied to me, that's hardly my concern. Come on, she was being well paid for her trouble. How many students get to earn five thousand pounds for four weeks' work?'

'That five thousand pounds is a fat lot of

good to her now.'

Dr Potter's face distorted into another smile as he said, 'I apologize for having to correct you, Mrs Pargeter, but might I suggest that "a *thin* lot of good" is a more appropriate expression?'

He laughed drily, demonstrating the huge gulf between his sensibilities and those of normal human beings.

'How much did anyone else know of what you were doing, Dr Potter?'

'Very little. Mr Arkwright didn't want to know any details. He thought they might distress him . . . which indeed they might well have done. He just did what I asked of him without asking any questions.'

'Yes,' Ank agreed bitterly, 'and I feel pretty dreadful about the whole business now that —'

'Be quiet!' If Dr Potter had been looking for a demonstration of his power over Ankle-Deep Arkwright, nothing could have been more effective than the way those two little words brought instant silence. 'Of course, there were drawbacks to his complete ignorance. If Mr Arkwright had known more about my experiments, he wouldn't have investigated the dead girl's room and so inconveniently supplied you with the name of a real person, Mrs Pargeter.'

'Still, couldn't be helped. Generally speaking — until the last few days when I've been forced to keep him out of the way down here, Mr Arkwright has been very biddable. As I said, remarkable how ready people are to do as you wish, when you know enough about their criminal background. Though, as you pointed out, Mrs Pargeter . . . I don't have any dirt on you.'

'No.'

'So . . .' he continued, his voice growing ever silkier with menace, 'I can't be confident of buying *your* silence with my own, can I?'

'No,' she replied defiantly.

'Which means I may have to effect your silence by some other method . . .' Muddy eyes gazed thoughtfully at her.

The ambulance man with the gun volunteered, 'Blow her away, shall I?'

Dr Potter winced at this crudeness. 'No, for Heaven's sake. I don't want to have to dispose of a body with bullet-holes in it. No, I think some kind of "accident" may be more appropriate . . .'

'Like the one you arranged for Lindy Galton?' suggested Mrs Pargeter, determined to keep him talking for as long as possible.

'Dear me, no,' he replied fastidiously. 'I don't like repeating myself. Anyway, even the notoriously dim British police force might get suspicious if a second corpse were to succumb to the embrace of the Dead Sea Mud. But I think it should be an "accident", none the less . . .'

He mused for a moment, then looked at her with glee as a thought struck him. 'Of course, you are somewhat overweight, aren't you, Mrs Pargeter . . . ?'

'It's never worried me.'

'No, but no one's to know that. No one like a coroner, say. You wouldn't be the first' — he chose his word carefully — '*mature* woman to have died from over-exercising.'

'I don't take any exercise. I never have. You can't make me exercise.'

'Oh, but the beauty of the situation is that I can, Mrs Pargeter. I can.'

'But why should I be found in Brotherton Hall, anyway? I'm not booked in here or —'

'Mr Arkwright is extremely proficient at falsifying registration records,' oozed Dr Potter, 'as I believe you've already discovered.'

This was too much for Ank. 'No! I'm not going to be party to anything that hurts Mrs Pargeter! All right, I've done some stuff for you I wish I hadn't, but —'

He got no further. At a signal from Dr Potter, the ambulance man with the baseball bat swung it upwards to connect with the point of Ankle-Deep Arkwright's jaw. His body sprawled backwards to slump against the wall.

Stan the Stapler made a move forward, but he was caught in the hollow at the back of his neck by the butt of the other ambulance man's automatic. He too crumpled to the ground.

'You stay with them,' the doctor curtly ordered the one with the gun. 'You bring her,' he told the other.

Stowing his baseball bat under one arm, the ambulance man locked the other round Mrs Pargeter. She tried to struggle, but could do nothing against his superior strength.

'Where to?'

'The gym,' Dr Potter replied.

She realized just before they got there what he had in mind. Nothing so crude as hanging her from ropes or crushing her with weights. No, it would be the passive exerciser, the one that Kim had tried to lure her on to.

She could do nothing. She was not strong enough to break free and there seemed little point in screaming or arguing. She knew Dr Potter would be impervious to argument, and she didn't want to give him the satisfaction of seeing how terrified she really was.

So she submitted while towels were wrapped round her wrists and ankles to prevent marking by the ropes with which she was bound on to the passive exerciser's lounger-like surface.

'The first bit,' Dr Potter told her solicitously, 'you will not find unpleasant . . . quite relaxing, actually. After about half an hour your limbs'll start to ache and you'll begin to sweat. From then on the pull on your muscles will get harder and harder, and the strain on your heart will get greater and greater . . .'

'I'll be very surprised if you're still alive by four o'clock. We'll come back at six to remove the ropes . . . but don't comfort yourself with the idea that if you're still alive then you will have survived. This isn't a trial by ordeal, Mrs Pargeter, it's just a convenient way of killing you. So, in the unlikely event that you are still breathing at six o'clock . . . we'll finish you off.'

The two men backed away and Dr Potter, a satisfied smile on his parchment-like face, threw a switch on the passive exerciser's mounting. As he had promised, the first movements felt reassuring, soothing, even relaxing.

'And what a comfort it must be to you, Mrs Pargeter,' was his parting shot, 'to know that you will die having lost an enormous amount of weight.'

Dr Potter let out an abrupt laugh; then he and the ambulance man left the gym.

Mrs Pargeter felt her unresistant body fold and unfold to the relentless rhythm of the exerciser. The sensation was still almost obscenely pleasant, but she knew that it would not long remain so.

Chapter Thirty-Seven

She was extremely annoyed. Not at the prospect of dying. That, Mrs Pargeter knew, had been an option from the moment of her birth, and life with the late Mr Pargeter, though wonderfully fulfilling, had kept the possibility of sudden death ever to the forefront of her mind.

No, it was the manner of her proposed dying that offended her. For Mrs Pargeter to end her days on an exercise machine was just so out of character. Of course, no one who knew her would ever imagine that she had got on to the thing voluntarily, but there might be people less familiar with her who thought the death was for real, who imagined that she, like many others of her age, had expired in an ill-judged attempt to recapture her lost youth. It was that thought she couldn't tolerate.

Still, it didn't seem she was going to have a lot of choice in the matter. The seductively soothing motion of the passive exerciser was now becoming more stressful. The machine itself had not accelerated — it maintained the inexorable evenness of its rhythm — but Mrs Pargeter's unaccustomed limbs were beginning to feel the strain. With each rise and fall she could sense a mounting tension in her shoulders and a regular tug at the back of her knees. Sweat had started to trickle into all the crevices of her body.

Not only was it an inappropriate death, Mrs Pargeter thought ruefully, it was also an extremely cruel one. A death that would take such a long time, apart from anything else, slowly sapping her body's strength, slowly winding up the tension around her heart.

'This is not the way I want to go!' she shouted suddenly. 'I would like it known that this is not the way I want to go!'

She felt better for saying it. Not that she deluded herself anyone might hear her. The gym was a long way away from the bedrooms in which the righteous guests of Brotherton Hall dreamed of self-indulgence. There was no chance of rescue. But she still felt better for saying it.

Given that she had time on her hands before she died — or before the welcome intervention of unconsciousness — Mrs Pargeter took the opportunity for a quick mental review of her life.

Couldn't complain, really. Except for this bloody death making the ending all untidy, it had been a good life. And an exciting one, thanks to the late Mr Pargeter. Also, thanks to the same benefactor, an emotionally fulfilled one. She had known the beauty of a truly balanced marriage, in which each partner loved the other equally, without inhibition or competition. Many people had to be content with far less.

And, as a bonus to the great central relationship of her life, she'd always been surrounded with friends. The value of devotion from someone like Truffler Mason was something she could never overestimate. And Truffler was only one of many associates of the late Mr Pargeter who'd made it their business to protect and cherish his widow.

It was a comfort too, before the end, to have had her suspicions of Ankle-Deep Arkwright and Stan the Stapler dissipated. The late Mr Pargeter really had commanded extraordinary loyalty.

Except in one quarter.

Julian Embridge.

Yes, as the last sands trickled through the hourglass of her life, that was Mrs Pargeter's one regret. Would have been nice to bring Julian Embridge to justice before she snuffed it.

Still, she reflected philosophically, can't have everything.

A door clicked gently open behind her.

Mrs Pargeter tried craning round to see who had come in, but the strapping impeded her.

She heard the soft tread of approaching feet. Then, in the thin light diffused from the 'Exit' sign, she was aware of a human figure lowering over her. She looked up to see the dull blue gleam of a knife-blade in its outstretched hand.

'Told you I'd settle up with you one day, didn't I, Mrs Pargeter?'

Chapter Thirty-Eight

She recognized the voice and sobbed with relief, as Jack the Knife continued, 'Didn't know the chance'd come this quickly, though.'

Then he switched off the passive exerciser and knelt down to cut her bonds. 'You all right?'

'Yes,' she murmured, flexing the muscles of her arms and legs. Even after their short exposure to the motion of the machine, they felt strained and shaky. 'Fine,' she asserted. 'Just fine. What on earth brought you here, though, Jack? Just a happy coincidence?'

'Bit more than that,' the surgeon replied. 'Had a call from Truffler Mason just before he came down here with you. Said he was going to Brotherton Hall on what might turn out to be "pressing business" . . . if you know what that means . . . ?'

'I know,' said Mrs Pargeter. 'Truffler and Ank — and Stan the Stapler — are all imprisoned down in the cellars by Dr Potter and his heavies.'

'Yes, I did a quick recce before I came along here. Brought it all back,' he whispered excitedly, 'what it was like working with your husband in the old days. Oh, it was great back then. He was a wonderful man, Mrs Pargeter. A real life-enhancer — he lit up everything he touched.'

She nodded fondly, but realized this wasn't the moment for wistful elegies. 'We've got to save the others!' she hissed.

Jack the Knife nodded in the thin light and reached into his pocket. 'One for each of us. Think we should be able to jump them all right.'

Mrs Pargeter felt the cool bulk of an automatic pistol pressed into her palm. As a rule, she didn't like firearms — indeed, she didn't favour violence of any kind — but these were exceptional circumstances.

They moved noiselessly out of the gym, along she corridor, and down the stairs to the cellar entrance. Though presumably in his Harley Street practice he had little chance to practise them, Jack the Knife's skills of stealth and subterfuge showed no signs of rustiness. He drew back the cellar door without a sound and beckoned Mrs Pargeter to follow him down.

'When we get there, I'm going to shoot out the light and catch them off guard.' He drew a large rubber covered torch from his pocket. 'Then switch this on. That should give us the advantage. I'll deal with the two thugs. You keep Dr Potter covered.'

'No problem,' Mrs Pargeter breathed back.

'And if he tries anything, just pull the trigger. Will you have any difficulty about doing that?'

'No,' she replied, with a certitude whose instinctiveness surprised her.

They moved silently downwards. With each step Mrs Pargeter felt the strain at the back of her knees, a chilling reminder that it really wouldn't have taken long for the exerciser to exhaust her totally.

Along the passage some way ahead light spilled from the room where their friends were held and, as they approached, they could hear the icy precision of Dr Potter's voice outlining his plans for the prisoners.

'. . . particularly convenient since the drugs require further testing — and on a more robust body than that of a young girl. Mr Mason here will be an ideal candidate for the treatment.'

'But, Doctor,' Ankle-Deep Arkwright's voice protested, 'those drugs have already killed one girl. Surely you don't want Truffler Mason to — ?'

'Truffler Mason has caused me considerable inconvenience,' Dr Potter snapped back. 'He's lucky I haven't just killed him straight off. At least with what I'm proposing, he has a chance of survival.'

'Not much of a chance.'

'No, Mr Arkwright, not much of a chance,' the doctor conceded with a hint of humour.

Mrs Pargeter wondered why Truffler was silent during this exchange, and concluded that he was probably still unconscious. As she and Jack the Knife edged closer, this conjecture was confirmed by the sight of Truffler's body still stretched out on the cellar floor.

Ankle-Deep Arkwright maintained his protest. 'I don't think you should do it, Doctor. There's been enough destruction here. I never wanted to be part of this in the first place. I —'

'Mr Arkwright!' Dr Potter interrupted malignantly. 'You will do as you're told. Either we get back to the arrangement we had before — that you run Brotherton Hall and do whatever I ask of you whenever I ask it — or I inform the police of your criminal past. And the same goes for you, Stan.'

'But I can't stand any more of this killing. First there's the student kid, then Lindy Galton, and if you've done anything to Mrs Pargeter, there are people all over the world who worked with her husband and will revenge her, whatever —'

'Mr Arkwright! If I cannot count on your

co-operation, then I will put you on the same medical programme as Mr Mason. My product still needs a lot more testing, you know.'

There was a chill silence as the impact of these words sank in, and Jack the Knife seized his cue.

A gunshot sounded, shatteringly loud in the enclosed space. Then came the smashing of glass, followed by a muddle of curses in the blackness.

By the time Jack the Knife had switched his torch on, half the job was done. Ankle-Deep Arkwright and Stan the Stapler, well trained by the late Mr Pargeter, had taken advantage of the confusion to immobilize the two ambulance men, who found themselves looking down the barrel of Jack the Knife's gun.

And in the spill of light from the torch, Dr Potter and Mrs Pargeter faced each other, machine-gun and automatic pistol trained.

'I will have no hesitation in using this,' he announced silkily.

'Nor will I in using this.'

'Do you know the rate at which this machine-gun pumps out bullets, Mrs Pargeter?'

'No. And I'm not particularly interested. It'll only take one bullet from my gun to blow you away, Dr Potter. I'm not going to miss from this range.'

There was a momentary impasse. Nobody moved, or seemed to breathe.

Then the doctor spoke again, his voice corroded with bitterness. 'I haven't come this far, I haven't come through everything to get so close to recognition as a brilliant chemist, to be thwarted by you. You're in my way, Mrs Pargeter, and when there's someone in my way, I always succeed in getting them out of my way!'

He concluded the sentence as if it were a cue — presumably a cue to squeeze the trigger of his machine-gun and blow Mrs Pargeter out of his way.

But the cue was missed. There was a sudden movement from the floor. Truffler Mason, with surprising athleticism, arched his body and brought his legs up to send the machine-gun spinning. The impact hurled Dr Potter back against the wall, where his head slammed against a low pipe. He crumpled unconscious to the floor.

'Brilliant, Truffler!' Mrs Pargeter gazed fondly down at her protector, who sat on the floor lugubriously rubbing his head.

Jack the Knife looked across at the two ambulance men, dispirited in the unyielding embraces of Ankle-Deep Arkwright and Stan the Stapler. Any fight there had been in the thugs was gone. 'Tie them up,' he ordered.

Then the surgeon moved across to focus his torchbeam on Dr Potter. He noticed something behind the man's ear and looked closer.

'Good Heavens!' he murmured.

'What is it?' asked Mrs Pargeter.

'These scars behind his ears.'

'What about them?'

'Just that I recognize them.'

'Hm?'

'A surgeon always recognizes his own handiwork, Mrs Pargeter.' Jack the Knife pushed Dr Potter's head sideways and peered closely at the network of lines around his eyes. 'Good God! Do you know who this is?'

'No?'

'Julian Embridge.'

Chapter Thirty-Nine

Hell had no fury like Mrs Pargeter in pursuit of justice. Shylock was not more pertinacious in his demands than she in her determination to settle scores with Julian Embridge.

The three villains were tied up to cellar pipes as Ankle-Deep Arkwright had been. 'Dr Potter' was still unconscious as he was manacled and Jack the Knife inspected his body, first removing the man's shoes.

'Look at this.' He pointed to the heavily built-up sole. 'Made him a good three inches taller.'

'Which explains why his body looked so out of proportion,' said Mrs Pargeter. And also, she thought to herself, why he refused to take his shoes off when he removed the body of the girl he'd killed from the Dead Sea Mud Bath.

'The hair's dyed, obviously,' Jack the Knife observed, 'and he had coloured lenses over his blue eyes . . .'

'Which is why they looked that strange muddy colour.'

'Yes, Mrs Pargeter. And all that, with the

work I'd done on him, was sufficient to change his basic appearance. The surgeon paused and looked puzzled. 'But there's more to it than that. I mean, Julian Embridge was a short, tubby person. This isn't the body of a short, tubby person.'

Mrs Pargeter smiled a bleak smile. 'I don't think we have to look far for the explanation, Jack. Think of the drug "Dr Potter" has been trying to develop, the drug that killed that poor girl. I think he was his own first guinea pig.'

Jack the Knife slowly nodded agreement as she went on, 'His background was as a chemist. He always had ambitions to produce something that would make him famous. The need to change his identity gave him the perfect incentive to experiment. But clearly the side-effects of whatever he developed meant that he couldn't put it straight on to the market. He needed to test it first and maybe he had suffered so much from earlier versions that he decided to try the drug out on other guinea pigs . . .'

'Hence the *Private Eye* small ad and all of that . . .'

'Yes.'

The surgeon looked thoughtful. 'Mind you, if he ever had developed it — a drug that could change basic body type — the slimming industry would have killed to get hold of it.'

'Unfortunate choice of phrase in the circumstances, Jack.'

'Yes. Sorry.'

'But it explains Sue Fisher's interest.' Mrs Pargeter pursed her lips. 'Hm, I'd really like to get Sue Fisher too . . .' But no, Ellie Fenchurch had made a deal with the creator of *Mind Over Fatty Matter*. Sue Fisher could not be implicated unless she broke her side of that bargain.

'Never mind,' Mrs Pargeter concluded easily. 'Julian Embridge is the important one. He's who I really want to get.'

'And how are you going to get him?' asked Jack the Knife.

'He's a criminal,' she replied primly. 'I'm going to turn him over to the police.'

Mrs Pargeter usually kept her dealings with the police to a minimum. She had no disrespect for the force, and was frequently heard to praise them as 'a fine body of men'. But she never liked causing unnecessary confusion. She was often of the opinion that an excess of information could only serve to make the constabulary's life more complicated.

And she was a model citizen in the sense that, rather than overburdening an already stretched force with problems that other people might have taken to their door, she usually sorted out such matters for herself (with the help of the late Mr Pargeter's associates).

But there were some cases in which she recognized that the police should be involved. And Julian Embridge's was such a case.

For one thing, the man was a public menace. People who go around illicitly testing drugs on young girls — and committing murder — deserve to be put away for a long time.

There was also a personal score to settle. It was through the offices of Julian Embridge at Streatham that the late Mr Pargeter had had a closer encounter with the British police force than he had wished for.

It was only fitting, therefore, that Julian Embridge should become a victim of the same authorities.

So, once the three villains had been secured in the cellar, with Stan the Stapler left to guard them, Mrs Pargeter and the others went upstairs to Ankle-Deep Arkwright's office. Truffler Mason, who spent much of his time as a private investigator typing up reports for clients, was seated behind the word processer, while he and Jack the Knife searched their memories for details of Julian Embridge's wrongdoing.

These recollections were rigorously edited by Mrs Pargeter. Nothing was allowed to appear in the text that could not be incontrovertibly proved. For example, the suspicion that Julian Embridge had taken on the identity of the doctor from Hong Kong, and might even have done away with the real Dr Potter, was not admitted. Only crimes that could be proved, and for which reliable witnesses could be quoted, were allowed to feature.

But there was still plenty of material. Enough to put Julian Embridge away for a very long time indeed.

Once the deposition had been completed, it would be faxed to the police. They would be given an untraceable fax number (a facility which Truffler Mason had developed and frequently used) to respond to if they were interested. Given the long list of crimes Truffler was keying in to the word processor, the police would quite definitely be interested. When they contacted the untraceable fax number, details of the whereabouts of Julian Embridge and his accomplices would be then faxed back to them.

Unfortunately, the two murders could not be included in the accusations. Jenny Hargreaves' body was still missing, and Lindy Galton's death seemed to have been passed off successfully as an accident.

'Pity about that,' said Mrs Pargeter, looking over Truffler Mason's shoulder at the screen.

'I'd really like to nail him for those.'

'Well, we could put in that the two deaths might be worth further investigation . . ?' Truffler suggested.

'What, and leave the police to try and get to the bottom of them?' Mrs Pargeter wrinkled her mouth sceptically. 'I'd feel safer if we could give them a bit of specific direction for their enquiries. Police're never that good when they have to use their own initiative.'

'No,' Jack the Knife agreed.

'What about Stan?' asked Ankle-Deep Arkwright suddenly. 'Might he know anything?'

'Good thinking,' Jack the Knife enthused. 'I'll go and get him.'

The oddjob man appeared a few minutes later, the surgeon having stayed downstairs on guard. Mrs Pargeter explained the information they required and he responded enthusiastically. Although Stan the Stapler couldn't speak, he could write. And he wrote furiously.

It was better than they'd dared hope. He had actually, unbeknownst to the perpetrator, witnessed 'Dr Potter' hitting Lindy Galton over the head and holding her under the Dead Sea Mud until she was dead.

And now he knew that the murderer had been Julian Embridge, Stan would be prepared to do anything to bring him to justice — even risk revelation of his own criminal background by standing up in court and bearing witness against the man who had betrayed the late Mr Pargeter.

'And what about Jenny Hargreaves?' asked Mrs Pargeter. 'Have you got any information on her death?'

The oddjob man looked at her in bewilderment.

'Jenny Hargreaves,' Ank explained. 'You know, the girl whose body was taken out on the trolley by Embridge's heavies. She'd died of the drug. Jenny Hargreaves.'

Stan still looked blank, so Ankle-Deep Arkwright continued, 'You must remember. Look, I didn't know she was here. Dr Potter kept all that stuff to himself. But after Mrs Pargeter told me about seeing the body, I went up to the room and checked, and found all these belongings with the name "Jenny Hargreaves" on them.'

'And then you falsified her registration details,' Mrs Pargeter observed coolly.

The manager coloured. 'Yes, look, I'm sorry. I did a lot of stuff I regret. I'm not proud of any of it, but I was just basically scared of Dr Potter. He'd got all this dirt on my criminal record — of course, now I know who he really is, I can see how he got it, but I still —'

'Never mind all that,' said Mrs Pargeter.

'We need to find out if Stan knows anything about Jenny Hargreaves' death.'

Ankle-Deep Arkwright was relieved to turn his attention back to the oddjob man. 'Look, you must know something about it, Stan. Mrs Pargeter saw you helping those two thugs put the body in the ambulance.'

Stan the Stapler shook his head and gurgled excitedly.

'What's he trying to say, Ank?' asked Mrs Pargeter.

'I don't know.'

'He's beckoning us to go with him,' said Truffler.

They followed the man back down to the cellars. He was almost running in his excitement, and the others exchanged puzzled looks as they hurried after him.

Once in the cellars, Stan the Stapler ignored the room where the three villains were imprisoned and hurried on to the end of the passage. He stopped outside a locked door and produced a key from his pocket. The door opened. He switched on the light and stepped aside to let Mrs Pargeter enter.

The room was clean but meagrely furnished. From a bed against the far wall a girl looked up blearily, her sleep broken by the sudden light.

She was very thin, but very much alive. Her

hair could have done with a wash, but was not falling out.

Mrs Pargeter felt a warm glow spreading inside her as she asked, 'Are you Jenny Hargreaves?'

Puzzled, the girl nodded.

Chapter Forty

It was a time of happy reunions.

Mrs Pargeter effected the first at Greene's Hotel. Jenny Hargreaves, remarkably unscathed by her incarceration, was seated over a large tea with lots of cream cakes when Truffler Mason, who had once again tracked down the young man, introduced Tom O'Brien.

Mrs Pargeter was deeply moved to see how they fell into each other's arms, and little surprised later when she heard that the young couple had impulsively married and would complete their degrees as man and wife. It gave her an inward smile to think how much Chloe, Candida, and Chris would disapprove, and a bigger smile to know how wrong their disapproval would be.

Tom, having once entertained the thought of losing Jenny, was now determined to cling on to her for ever. First things first — changing the world could wait. And in time, no doubt, her parents would come round to the idea of him.

The discovery of Jenny alive did of course

raise the question of whose body Mrs Pargeter had seen removed from Brotherton Hall in the small hours, and she had to wait until Julian Embridge's trial to find the answer to that question.

It was answered, though, in meticulous detail, because the two ambulance men, desperate to save as much of their own skins as they could, testified against their employer. They provided chapter and verse on the death of a girl, as well as where her body was hidden, and they furnished details of many more offences by Julian Embridge than Mrs Pargeter's deposition had managed to muster.

The dead girl had been another student, recruited in the same way as Jenny Hargreaves. Mrs Pargeter felt appropriate sympathy for the girl's parents, but the death touched her only in the generalized way of tragedy reported in a newspaper. Whereas with Jenny, although she only met the girl at the end of the ordeal, she had felt personally involved.

The ambulance men also shopped their employer for the murder of Lindy Galton, thus saving Stan the Stapler the potential embarrassment of standing up in court.

The outcome of the trial was very satisfactory all round, and the chances of Julian Embridge ever leaving prison alive were extremely remote.

His betrayal of the late Mr Pargeter was avenged. Mrs Pargeter had her pound of flesh.

The fact that justice, though blind, can sometimes be unerringly accurate was also demonstrated in the case of Sue Fisher.

Ellie Fenchurch was true to their agreement and breathed not a word of what she knew about *Mind Over Fatty Matter*. Until the day she heard that Sue Fisher had actually tried to persuade Lord Barsleigh to sack his controversial interviewer.

The deal was broken, the gloves were off, and Ellie Fenchurch published an interview so scalding that it made all her previous character-assassinations seem benign by comparison.

Sue Fisher immediately mustered her lawyers, but the coincident start of the Julian Embridge trial made their task well-nigh impossible. The connection between the experiments of 'Dr Potter' and *Mind Over Fatty Matter* was quickly public knowledge, and Sue Fisher's empire began to crumble.

This collapse probably would have happened even without the scandal. Food and fitness fads have brief lives and, even before Ellie Fenchurch's revelations, the latest *Mind Over Fatty Matter* book had been pipped to the top of the bestsellers' lists by a new slimming sensation, *The Wrist and Ankle Diet.*

The author of this volume was quick to capitalize on her success (homing in, exactly as Sue Fisher had done, on the communal guilt of women about the state of their bodies). She set up a chain of *Wrist and Ankle* Exercise Clinics all over the country. She marketed videos of herself flexing her wrists and ankles; and entered into merchandizing deals, first for designer *Wrist and Ankle* weights, but very quickly thereafter for *Wrist and Ankle* leotards, leggings, and exercise bras. *Wrist and Ankle* Cuisine was not far behind, and an infinite vista stretched ahead of *Wrist and Ankle* fabrics, furniture, domestic appliances, and lawnmowers.

Mind Over Fatty Matter leisurewear began to be sold at discounted prices in street markets, and given as birthday presents to teenage girls by elderly aunts. The writing was on the wall for Sue Fisher.

Her fall was as swift as her rise. Because she had made no friends on the way up, none stepped forward to slow her downward trajectory.

She rescued enough money from the wreckage to buy a villa in Majorca, where she retired alone. She developed a taste for Bailey's Irish Cream, and grew fat.

* * *

Ankle-Deep Arkwright, anticipating the end of the fitness boom, converted Brotherton Hall into a Gastronomic Centre, where he ran a series of horrendously expensive themed Weekend Breaks ('The Taste of France', 'The Taste of Spain', 'The Taste of Italy', etc.). The chef Gaston reverted to his real name of 'Nitty' Wilson and was in seventh heaven.

The Weekend Breaks became very popular amongst food snobs, who relished the exclusivity of Brotherton Hall. Competition developed amongst them to see who could be first to extract a single word from the Gastronomic Centre's incredibly standoffish *maitre d'hotel*. This contest continued for years without anybody realizing that Stan the Stapler was dumb.

Ankle-Deep Arkwright was very insistent that Mrs Pargeter should come regularly to Brotherton Hall and try out each new theme and, when other commitments permitted, she was happy to oblige.

Jack the Knife also offered her the full range of his professional services, but these, with her customary charm, she declined.

The Friday after the unmasking of Julian Embridge, Mrs Pargeter witnessed another happy reunion.

The little house in Catford was full of Kim and small girls and poodles and Mrs Moore and all the cream cakes that Mrs Moore had made for the great homecoming, but it was even fuller of Thicko Thurrock.

Mrs Pargeter had forgotten how huge he was, and indeed how much the little house had missed the reassurance of his bulk. As one of the girls ushered her in, Thicko grinned from his armchair, where he sat with his arms round Kim.

'Sorry not to get up, Mrs P. Got a lot of cuddling to catch up on.'

And he grinned at his wife with such devotion that Mrs Pargeter's heart gave a little sob. 'Looking great, isn't she?' he said proudly as his hands wandered over Kim's familiar contours. 'Triffic. Needs to put a bit of weight on, mind. Been pining for me, hasn't she? Still, soon fatten her up, won't we, eh? Come on, Mother, you give Mrs P. a glass of the old bubbly. And a bit of that cake, eh?'

'Nice to be home then, Thicko?' asked Mrs Pargeter as she subsided into a chair, quickly to be engulfed by small girls and poodles.

'I'll say. Nice to see everyone.' He gave his wife a hug. 'Ooh, I missed ya, Kim.' His hand traced the curve of her bottom. 'You know, it's really nice having a wife with the best bum in the business.'

Kim Thurrock giggled with delight and coyly avoided Mrs Pargeter's eye.

Later, as the champagne flowed, Mrs Pargeter needed to go up to the bathroom. On the floor were Kim's scales.

With a grin at her reflection in the mirror, Mrs Pargeter kicked off her shoes and stepped on to the platform. She looked at the dial.

Eleven stone four pounds.

'Yes, that's about right,' said Mrs Pargeter comfortably.

The employees of THORNDIKE PRESS hope you have enjoyed this Large Print book. All our Large Print books are designed for easy reading — and they're made to last.

Other Thorndike Large Print books are available at your library, through selected bookstores, or directly from us. Suggestions for books you would like to see in Large Print are always welcome.

For more information about current and upcoming titles, please call or mail your name and address to:

THORNDIKE PRESS
PO Box 159
Thorndike, Maine 04986
800/223-6121
207/948-2962